'Richard... w
insane!'

'Yes, we should. A
more than I've wanted anything in the past
eight years and you do too. Don't you? Admit
it, Emma; tell me that you want me. Say it!'

'I want you, Richard,' she breathed. Oh, how
she wanted him!

'That's all I needed to know,' he said coldly.

And, to Emma's astonishment and chagrin,
Richard rose to his feet.

'Goodnight, Emma.'

Dear Reader

The new year is a time for resolutions and here at Mills & Boon we will continue to give you the best romances we possibly can. We're sure the year's books will live up to your expectations! This month we hope to shake off the winter chills by taking you to some wonderful exotic locations—Morocco, the Bahamas and the Caribbean. Closer to home, this is the time of year when we celebrate love and lovers, with St Valentine's Day. Which of our heroes would you like to spend the day with? Until next month,

The Editor

Angela Devine grew up in Tasmania surrounded by forests, mountains and wild seas, so she dislikes big cities. Before taking up writing, she worked as a teacher, librarian and university lecturer. As a young mother and Ph.D. student, she read romantic fiction for fun and later decided it would be even more fun to write it. She is married with four children, loves chocolate and Twinings teas and hates ironing. Her current hobbies are gardening, bushwalking, travelling and classical music.

Recent titles by the same author:

MISSISSIPPI MOONLIGHT

YESTERDAY'S HUSBAND

BY
ANGELA DEVINE

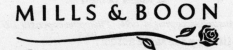

MILLS & BOON

MILLS & BOON LIMITED
ETON HOUSE, 18-24 PARADISE ROAD
RICHMOND, SURREY TW9 1SR

To Kirk, whose eyes are the colour
of a storm-tossed sea.

*MILLS & BOON and the Rose Device
are trademarks of the publisher.*

*First published in Great Britain 1994
by Mills & Boon Limited*

© Angela Devine 1994

*Australian copyright 1994   Philippine copyright 1995
This edition 1995*

ISBN 0 263 78874 1

Set in Times Roman 10 on 11¼ pt.
01-9502-57051 C

Made and printed in Great Britain

CHAPTER ONE

As THE hotel bus bowled along through the lush green Balinese countryside, Emma Prero felt a wave of nostalgia so powerful that she caught her breath. The Indonesian island was every bit as magical and exotic as her memories of her honeymoon had told her. Graceful palm trees waved their feathery green foliage overhead, monkeys scuttled in alarm up the mossy green walls of stone temples, girls in colourful tie-dyed skirts and blouses strolled along the roadside verges with baskets of fruit balanced on their heads. Once the driver was forced to come to a complete halt when a flock of noisy, squabbling ducks spread right across the road. As he opened the door to shout a protest at their owner, a warm rush of tropical air filled the vehicle's air-conditioned interior. It brought with it the unmistakable scent of the island, a dense, intoxicating compound of moist sea breezes, frangipani blooms and Eastern spices. Breathing in that distinctive fragrance, Emma was hit by a sharp, painful longing for Richard. The sensation was so vivid that she shut her eyes briefly, almost expecting to find him sitting beside her just as he had done nine long years before. But there was no warm, muscular thigh next to hers, no large, calloused hand brushing her fingers, no rumble of masculine laughter beside her. When she opened her eyes again, the seat was empty and the door of the bus was closing with a soft hiss. Emma gripped her Gucci handbag and took a deep, shuddering breath, trying to control the wild beating of her heart. Why did I come? she wondered in panic. I must have been crazy!

5

Do I really want to inflict this kind of pain on myself? It was a stupid idea. Stupid, stupid, stupid!

Turning her head away from the window, she glanced at the other occupants of the bus. But that only made her feel worse. In front of her were two elderly couples with silvery hair and cheerful, smiling faces, who looked as if they were still on their honeymoons forty years after the wedding. Behind her she could hear a large assortment of excited young people, already striking up friendships. And directly opposite her was the most painful sight of all. A genuine honeymoon couple. The woman still had scraps of confetti in her long, curly auburn hair and she was gazing with luminous happiness at her new husband. As for him, he seemed to be oblivious of everything except his bride's liquid brown eyes. The sight sent a pain like a knife twisting through Emma's heart. She couldn't be much older than them in years—after all, she was only twenty-eight—but she felt centuries beyond them in bitter experience. Sighing, she unscrewed the crumpled colour travel brochure which she had been thoughtlessly mangling, and tried to read it. It was no use complaining. She had made her own bed and now she must lie on it.

There was another bad moment as the bus pulled up in the leafy courtyard of the hotel. Following the luggage porter into the dim, cool interior, she heard the sound of a gamelan orchestra. The strange, percussive music with its drums and cymbals and bronze pots held a thrilling dissonance that was instantly and hauntingly familiar. Yes, there had been an orchestra just like that when she and Richard had signed in at this very desk nine years ago. It was the first time she had used her married name and her fingers had shaken as she'd taken the pen in her hand. They were shaking again now and her writing came out spidery and illegible.

'Emma Fielding.'

The name looked strange to her, for she had barely used it in the eight years since she and Richard parted. Yet some foolish impulse had made her leave it on her passport, so that when she travelled she still had the illusion of being genuinely married. The same foolish impulse had prevented her from ever asking Richard for a divorce. Although she told herself that she despised him, it gave her a hollow, aching kind of comfort to pretend that one day they might get back together. Pigs might fly! she told herself savagely, setting down the pen. Richard would go to the moon sooner than have anything further to do with me. Her lips twisted at the thought.

'You do not look happy, madam,' said the desk clerk, his almond-shaped eyes narrowing in concern. 'Is something wrong?'

'No, no,' Emma assured him in a stifled voice. *Just that my husband hates me, I'm on the verge of going bankrupt to the tune of twenty million dollars and I'm so miserable I wish I'd never been born.* 'Nothing important.'

The man smiled warmly at her, displaying perfect white teeth.

'Ah, you travel alone. Perhaps you are lonely, yes? Allow me to make a suggestion. Every night we have a cabaret in the Arjuna Room, very friendly, very informal. Lots of Balinese dancing, very happy for our guests. There will be many young people there. Perhaps you like me to put you at a table with some other tourists so you can make friends?'

Emma winced inwardly. The last thing she wanted was to sit with a group of total strangers in a holiday mood. But the clerk was so earnest, so genuinely anxious to help that she felt she owed him some kind of explanation.

'Er... that's very kind of you,' she said, inventing wildly, 'but I'm rather tired from the plane trip and in any case I probably won't be alone for long. My husband may be arriving later in the evening, so I'd rather stay in my room and wait for him.'

'Of course, of course, madam. I understand. I will look out for him.'

Well, you'll be looking for a long time, thought Emma as she took the key with a wry smile. But when a bellboy in a black sarong, vividly printed scarlet shirt and batik headscarf came forward to take her bag, she felt her spirits lift unexpectedly. As she followed him along the highly polished teak floors through a maze of corridors, the depression of the last few months began to ebb away from her. Perhaps it had been a good idea to come on this trip, after all. With a shock she realised that it was the first holiday she had taken since she left Richard.

The bellboy opened a glass door leading to the outside of the building and ushered her on to a shady veranda. Once again she experienced that heady waft of warm, moist, tropical air. Her companion's sandals scuffed softly on the crazy paving of the path as he led her between low, clipped hedges that bordered a garden filled with ginger lilies, hibiscus and frangipani bushes.

'There, madam,' he said, pointing to a building directly in front of them. 'That is your bungalow. And the closest swimming-pool is just through the stone gateway on the right.'

In spite of being called a bungalow, the building in front of Emma was actually two storeys high and built in the traditional native style. It had a high gabled roof covered in orange pantiles, the walls were covered in orange rendering with inset panels of carved grey stone and the shady verandas both upstairs and downstairs were scattered with invitingly deep, cushioned bamboo chairs. She found her thoughts turning immediately to long, cool, fruity drinks clinking with ice.

'Come in, come in,' urged the bellboy, smiling. 'Nice and cool inside.'

It was nice and cool. The air-conditioning purred softly and the room that met her gaze was tastefully furnished and welcoming. Against the neutral cream walls hung vividly coloured Balinese paintings of landscapes and mythological scenes. A Barong mask with intricately decorated gold ears, bulging eyes and monstrous teeth grinned wickedly above an ornately carved teak drinks cabinet. The actual furniture was minimal—a comfortable lounge suite covered in green batik, a couple of bamboo coffee-tables and a bamboo dining suite. But behind a magnificently carved wooden screen the bellboy pointed out a tiny, fully equipped kitchen. Then he led her up the stairs to the bedroom.

Here the memories were so sharp that they were almost a physical pain. As she looked around every detail seemed to be etched vividly in her memory. The two vast beds with their exuberant bedspreads writhing with brilliant tropical flowers, the paintings of courting egrets on the walls, the carved dressing-tables and wardrobes were all unbearably familiar. Even the bathroom with its gold taps and green marble fittings was a poignant reminder of the past. All the same, as the bellboy deposited her suitcase and pointed out the various features of the room to her she tried to smile. Yet the only thing she wanted now was to be left in peace, alone with her memories.

'Thank you very much,' she said at last, gently cutting him off by handing him a five thousand rupiah note. 'If you could have some iced juice and fruit sent over to me soon, I'd be grateful.'

When his thanks had died away and the door downstairs had closed quietly, she was finally free to stop keeping up appearances. Kicking off her shoes with a sigh of relief, she delved into the thick chignon at the back of her head, yanked out the hairpins and felt her long hair tumble loose around her shoulders. Then, driven by another of her absurd impulses, she wrestled her suitcase up on to the bed and rummaged inside it. At last she found what she was looking for and laid it out on the bedspread. With shaking fingers she pulled off everything—her expensive French suit with the gold brooch on the lapel, her silk tights, hand-embroidered underwear, pearl necklace and gold pearl drop-earrings. Then she picked up the long, wrap-around batik dress which Richard had bought her on their honeymoon. It was a smoky blue colour with a halter neck, no back whatsoever from the waist up, a long, swirling skirt and a red starburst of colour like the explosion of a supernova on the front. The smell of the sandalwood chest where she had kept it all these years rose faintly to her nostrils as she tied it around her. Picking up a hairbrush, she attacked her hair with long, jerky, tugging strokes, but flung the brush aside before she had finished. A small, stark smile distorted her lips as she walked slowly across to the dressing-table mirror.

'You haven't changed much, Em,' she said to her reflection.

But the cynical narrowing of her eyes and the wry pursing of her mouth told her she was wrong. Oh, in one way it was true. With her wavy, dark hair cascading around her shoulders and her petite, almost adolescent figure, she still looked much like the nineteen-year-old girl Richard had married. Her pale, creamy skin was still fresh and unlined, while her small breasts were little more than a gentle swell beneath the thin fabric of her dress. Yet in other ways she was a woman, and an embittered woman at that. Her eyes, yellow-flecked at the centre and deep green around the outer edge of the irises, stared back at her with their habitual wary expression. And there was an indefinable tension in the whole carriage of her small, neat body.

'Oh, damn it!' she exclaimed. 'Why did I do this? I should have known there was no going back.'

Tearing off the gauzy Balinese dress, she opened the bathroom door and flung it down on the floor. Perhaps a shower would freshen her up and stop her being so ridiculously gloomy. After all, this holiday was supposed to be fun. A last fling, a chance to enjoy herself before the dreary, humiliating task of declaring herself bankrupt.

With a determined gesture, she slammed the door to the bedroom, turned on the taps and stepped under the shower. Deliberately she let it run quite cool, so that when she stepped under it she let out an involuntary squeal of shock. But after five minutes under that cool, invigorating hail, a sense of well-being began to invade her. I won't think about Richard any more, she told herself forcefully. I'll just relax, unwind and soak up the sun and the atmosphere. After that, I'll be in much better shape to tackle my problems.

Closing her eyes, she lifted her face to the downpour of cool water and shuddered luxuriously. Mmm, she was feeling better already. She turned off the taps, groped for a thick, fluffy towel and stepped out of the shower stall. As she wrung the water out of her hair, she thought she heard the distant sound of a door closing downstairs. Probably Room Service with the snack she had ordered. Well, she had better make herself decent in case the maid came upstairs. Rubbing herself briskly, she pulled on the flimsy Balinese dress, gave her hair a final wipe and dropped the towel. Then she opened the door, stepped into the bedroom and suffered a shock so appalling that her heart almost stopped.

'Richard,' she moaned.

It was him. Really him. Not some lunatic figment of her imagination like the fantasy on the bus, but a real, solid, breathing human being. As tall and broad as he always had been, with the same sun-streaked, curly blond hair, tanned skin and vivid blue eyes. But different. Oh, God, how different! He was still devastatingly good-looking, but there was a harshness about him that the younger Richard hadn't had. A brooding quality of power and authority that radiated out to meet her with devastating force. Like Emma, he was dressed in the sort of casual clothes they had worn on their honeymoon—in his case thin beige shorts and a beige and tan batik safari jacket which revealed his muscular legs and forearms. Yet the resemblance to the man she had once loved with all her heart ended with the clothes. In all other ways this was a stranger, who stood grim and unsmiling between the two huge beds, his stance and expression radiating an unmistakable hostility. But what on earth was he doing here?

'Hello, Emma.'

She clutched at the door-frame to support herself. His deep, throaty voice was unmistakable.

'What are you doing here?' she asked in a frozen whisper.

He seemed as unruffled by the question as if he had only left her ten minutes before to step out for a breath of fresh air. With a casual motion of his hand, he waved at the stairs.

'I'll explain in a moment,' he said serenely. 'In the meantime, why don't you come down and join me in a snack?'

A feeling of unreality took hold of Emma as she glided down the stairs behind him. Could this really be happening? It was outrageous, impossible! And yet the ornately carved teak banister felt disconcertingly firm under her fingers and the jug of iced juice accompanied by a platter of luscious, tropical fruit looked real enough. Sinking unsteadily into one of the cushioned chairs, she accepted a drink from Richard and carried it to her mouth with nerveless fingers. The sweet, fruity blend of pineapple, coconut, ice and milk flowed refreshingly into her mouth and gave her a little reassurance. No, she wasn't dreaming! All the same, her feelings were in turmoil at this unexpected sight of her husband after so many years apart. A swirl of questions whirled in her head like a cloud of coloured butterflies. Why, how, when? Without even stopping to think, she spoke.

'How did you know I was here?' she blurted out.

Richard shrugged, smiled and looked as if it had been the easiest thing in the world to find out Emma's whereabouts, even though they were supposed to be strictly secret. Picking up his own drink, he settled into the depths of one of the cushioned chairs.

'Miss Matty told me,' he said.

'Matty?' echoed Emma indignantly. 'You wormed the information out of Matty? I can't believe it! She's always been the perfect secretary, totally discreet. And I told her nobody was to know where I was.'

Richard gave a faint, mirthless laugh and raised his glass to her in a taunting salute.

'Well, perhaps she thought your husband was entitled to special treatment,' he said in a steely voice. 'Besides, I told her I had an important proposition which needed to be put to you immediately.'

'Proposition?' cried Emma in alarm. 'What kind of proposition? What do you mean?'

'Now don't be so hasty, Emma,' drawled Richard lazily. 'We've got a lot of catching up to do before we talk about that. It's a long time since we've seen each other.'

It certainly is, thought Emma, and her hand shook as she set down her glass. For one crazy moment she had felt an exhilarating uplift of joy at the sight of Richard, but now she saw how mistaken that reaction had been. There was nothing friendly in the brooding face that confronted her across the table and she felt absolutely no urge to catch up on what he had been doing in the time since she'd seen him last. In any case, she was all too bitterly aware of it. The glossy magazines and the financial journals had kept her informed of every detail of his meteoric rise to wealth and of the glamorous, sexy women who helped him to enjoy it. With a brief, aching sense of regret, she wished that she had never driven him away from her. Then she would never have had to endure the anguish of watching him find love and success without her. With a wry twist of her lips, Emma wondered whether Richard had followed her career and her supposed love life in the Press as thoroughly as she had followed his. His next words showed that he had.

'I'm not hypocrite enough to pretend that I was sorry to hear of your father's death,' he said bluntly. 'But I hope it wasn't painful.'

A shadow crossed her face as she thought of the agonising weeks she had spent in the private hospital at her father's bedside. Weeks when she would have given anything for the friendly touch of Richard's hand on her shoulder.

'It was,' she said hoarsely.

'I'm sorry. Liver cancer is a dreadful disease. But I've got to hand it to you, Emma. You showed a lot of guts in tackling it the way you did. I know you were close to your father and it must have been hell to see him die by inches. I also think you did an amazing job of taking over Prero's when you were only twenty-one.'

Emma felt surprised and grateful at this unexpected praise. Her pale cheeks flushed with colour and her eyes brightened.

'Th-thank you,' she stammered.

'Of course, the recession must have dealt you some pretty heavy blows since then,' continued Richard, scrutinising her shrewdly. 'Times haven't been easy to property developers, especially those with large office holdings in the central business district. Tell me, how is the company performing now in your view, Emma?'

The question shot out like a bullet from a gun and wounded Emma to the heart. For a moment she contemplated telling him the truth, but her pride wouldn't allow her to make such a humiliating confession of failure. Instead she forced a strained smile to her lips.

'Times haven't been easy,' she said glibly, 'but on the whole I think the company is doing very well indeed.'

With lazy, unhurried movements, Richard set down his glass and rose to his feet. Then, moving around the table, he leaned forward and caressed Emma's cheek with an enigmatic smile on his face.

'You're a barefaced liar, sweetheart,' he said softly.

Her senses reeled as if he had assaulted her. The double shock of his words and his touch were too much for her to deal with. The colour drained away from her cheeks and her heart began to pound violently. She tried twice to speak and failed. Then her words came out in a hoarse croak.

'You know?'

'Yes.'

Emma shuddered and flung back her head, feeling a terrible pain jolt through her entire body as if she really had been wounded. Shaking her head in a dazed fashion, she gave Richard a haunted look as he resumed his seat.

'Then I suppose the whole Sydney business community knows?' she demanded. Her throat felt so tight she could hardly force the words out.

'No,' replied Richard in measured tones. 'You've concealed matters well and, to your credit, I must say you ran a damned hard race to save the company. If the Sawford merchant bank hadn't failed, you might even have made it. As it is, you're at the end of your rope, aren't you?'

Emma shuddered again.

'Yes.'

Richard caressed his glass with a long brown finger, as sensually as if he were stroking a beautiful woman's neck.

'Just as a matter of interest,' he said, 'what are you doing on an expensive holiday when you're about to go bankrupt? Is there some good reason for it or is it just another one of your spoilt-little-rich-girl tricks?'

This lazy innuendo, delivered hot on the heels of the shock he had just dealt her, made Emma's over-strained temper snap. Leaping to her feet, she stared at him with flashing eyes and gritted teeth.

'Damn you!' she cried. 'Did you just come here to insult me?'

Awkwardly she sidled between the chair and the table, intent on putting as much distance as possible between herself and Richard. But as she emerged from the cluster of furniture his voice cracked through the air like a whiplash.

'Don't leave yet, Emma; we haven't finished.'

'Well, I'm finished with you,' she flared. 'You never could watch me spending money without carping about it, could you? And I don't suppose it makes a blind bit of difference to you that I could have a perfectly good reason for being here!'

'Such as?' he taunted, raising one eyebrow indolently.

Her body was shaking so much that she had to clutch the back of a chair for support. How could she tell him the truth? That the real reason she wanted to come here was because it was the one place on earth where she had once been perfectly happy. A happiness based on being with him. That was the last thing she wanted to admit to him now.

'I don't see that it's really any of your business,' she said. 'But if it's any comfort to you, I did feel guilty and worried about the thought of spending money on a holiday, although the few thousand dollars it cost for this would just be a drop in the ocean compared to the debts I'm going to owe very soon. But as a matter of fact I didn't pay for this holiday. It wasn't even my idea that I should take it. It was my mother's and she put up the money for it, not me.'

'Your mother?' echoed Richard in surprise. 'Do you mean you're seeing her these days? I thought good old Daddy had forbidden it.'

'Don't speak about my father in that hateful, sneering voice,' blazed Emma. 'I was twenty-one when he died, a grown woman. I know he and my mother were on bad terms after the divorce, but I felt I had to make my own choice about what I did.'

'I'm glad to hear it,' said Richard bitterly. 'It's a pity you didn't stand up to him on a few other issues, or maybe you wouldn't have stuffed up your life the way you did. You were certainly well and truly under his thumb when I knew you.'

'I wasn't!' cried Emma.

'Really? I beg to differ. In fact, I've always thought that if it hadn't been for good old Daddy maybe you wouldn't have jumped into bed with Nigel Wellings while you were still married to me.'

Emma's skin went cold and clammy with horror at this cruel reminder of the past.

'You bastard!' she hissed. 'You know damned well it didn't happen like that. Look, if you've just come here to insult me, it's a total waste of time. Now do me a favour, will you, and leave?'

'No,' said Richard softly.

'I'll have you thrown out!' threatened Emma.

He gave an unpleasant laugh.

'Really?' he taunted. 'Now that will be interesting. What will you tell the hotel staff when you ask them to come and throw me out? After all, darling, I'm your husband. You told the man at the desk you were expecting me tonight. He made a point of mentioning it to me when I asked about you. Won't it all be rather embarrassing for you?'

Emma shuddered and fell silent. The scene would not merely be embarrassing, it would be utterly unthinkable. But before she could say another word, Richard continued in a dangerously silky voice, 'So you've got a lover, have you? Well, I can't say that really surprises me, knowing you as I do. But I rather object to having him smuggled in under my name. Who is the lucky man anyway?'

'Nobody!' cried Emma. 'I only said that because they were offering to put me at a table with other tourists. I wanted a bit of privacy!'

Richard's even white teeth gritted together in a feral smile.

'I've told you once you're a barefaced liar,' he murmured. 'And now I'll say it again. I don't believe you.'

'Well, I can't care what you believe!' cried Emma in a voice shaking with rage. 'Because it's all over between us, isn't it? So why don't you just get out? Go on, get out!'

'Oh, no,' said Richard, still with that same dangerous smile. 'I'm not leaving till you've heard my proposition. You see, Emma, I just may be able to save you from bankruptcy.'

Emma's whole body felt suddenly cold and still.

'You'd do that?' she breathed. 'But why? I always thought you hated me.'

Richard's blue eyes narrowed shrewdly.

'Maybe I do, but I have my reasons. I'll tell you about them over dinner tonight. Of course, there'll be conditions.'

'Conditions?' said Emma in a high, frightened voice. 'What kind of conditions?'

Richard's fingers flexed and unflexed slowly as if he thought he was holding her in the palm of his hand.

'Conditions which I don't think you'll like,' he purred. 'But then that's part of being rich enough to call the tune, isn't it, Emma? You probably remember the pleasure of holding that kind of power, don't you, sweetheart? Now, what time would you like to eat? I'll tell you what. You put on your prettiest dress and I'll call for you at seven...'

After the door had closed quietly behind Richard's departing back, Emma sank down on one of the chairs in a daze of disbelief. So often in the past she had daydreamed fervently of the day when Richard would seek her out. Somehow all the festering hurts and long-standing bitterness that had sprung from their estrangement would be smoothed away and they would feel the same passionate love for each other that they had felt when they first met. But never in her wildest moments had she dreamt of a reunion like this one. Meeting Richard again so unexpectedly had shocked her beyond measure. And all the old wounds which she had thought healed, or at least numb, seemed to have broken open afresh. A raw, painful sense of humiliation assaulted her as she thought of this recent encounter. There had been no doubt whatsoever that Richard still hated her. Equally, something in the expression in his eyes told her there was no doubt that he still desired her. Just as she desired him. The shameful, humiliating fact was that she only had to look at him to experience a flood of pulsating warmth through her entire body. If only he had come back to her in love, not hatred, she felt certain that they would now be naked together in the big bed upstairs. Covering her face, she let out a low groan. Why had he come? Why? Why? Why? It made no sense. Why should he want to save Prero's from certain disaster? If he hated her, wouldn't it make more sense simply to let her sink without throwing her a line? And what sort of proposition did he have in mind?

She couldn't answer these questions and brooding over them only gave her a headache and a strong urge to burst into hysterics. Pulling herself together with an effort, she rose to her feet. There was no sense in worrying herself sick. It would be more sensible to go out for a swim, change into her best clothes and meet him at dinnertime on her own ground, as the hard-headed, cool businesswoman she had become in the past few years. Setting her lips grimly, she rummaged in her bag and found a large beach towel, a skimpy emerald-green bikini, sandals and a bottle of suntan lotion. Thus equipped, she made her way down to the pool.

The setting was idyllic and, if she had not been so upset by Richard's unexpected arrival, all her worries would have ebbed away at the sight of it. In fact, it wasn't just one pool but several winding in a serpentine pattern in and out of the landscaped gardens. Two or three changing-huts, open to the breeze and with orange tiled roofs, offered welcome shade, while carved stone elephants on the tiled surrounds of the pool squirted water from their upraised trunks. In the background a line of palm trees flailed like green windmills in the breeze from the ocean. Emma slipped out of the sarong that she was wearing over her bikini and dropped it on to a bench in one of the changing-huts. Then she slid into the deliciously warm, silky water. It was heavenly to lie back floating and stare up into the cloudless blue sky. If only Richard hadn't come, this would have been a marvellous vacation. Perhaps it still would be if only she could persuade him to go away and leave her in peace. For somehow she had an ominous sense of certainty that his proposal to save Prero's was going to come at a price that she wasn't prepared to pay.

She found out how accurate that presentiment had been when she and Richard met for dinner that evening. He arrived on the dot at seven o'clock looking coldly handsome in a lightweight white dinner-jacket, black trousers and white shirt. Emma had dressed equally carefully. Not because Richard had told her to put on her best clothes, but because the knowledge that she looked as glamorous as possible gave a badly needed boost to her confidence. She had swept her dark hair up into its usual chignon at the back and she was wearing a long frock of scarlet chiffon with a sweetheart neckline and a gold and pearl necklace around her throat. Tawny eyeshadow brought out the gold flecks in her eyes and a light touch of blusher high on her cheekbones concealed her pallor, while her lips were painted a defiant scarlet to match the dress. Richard gave her a small, ironical bow when she opened the door to him.

'Very attractive,' he commented.

'Thank you,' she said curtly. 'Shall we go?'

The restaurant was on the fifth floor of the main hotel building with a panoramic view over the ocean. The front door was flanked by two huge statues of fierce-looking Indonesian warriors intricately carved in stone and lit from below so that their eyes seemed to gleam wickedly. A smiling girl in a scarlet sarong came forward from behind a desk flanked by masses of greenery to ask their names.

'Mr and Mrs Fielding,' said Richard as casually as if they had been together for the past eight years.

'Of course, sir. Please come this way.'

The restaurant was dimly lit in order to take full advantage of the magnificent view over the ocean and Richard seemed to loom like a caveman beside her as they picked their way through the flickering candlelight.

At last the waitress showed them to a table discreetly secluded by an ornate carved screen from the rest of the room and with a superb view of the moonlit ocean far below. Emma felt as nervous and tongue-tied as if she were fifteen years old when Richard held out one of the cushioned bamboo chairs so that she could sit down. When he was seated too, the waitress spread large scarlet napkins on their laps and handed them each a menu.

'May I get you some pre-dinner drinks, sir?' she asked.

'Emma?'

'Oh, just a gin and tonic for me,' said Emma hastily.

She felt far too agitated at this moment to know or care what the local drinks were, although normally she was quite adventurous when it came to sampling regional specialities.

'That seems a bit tame,' said Richard, his eyebrows shooting up. 'I'll try the arak cocktail myself. But I do hope you are going to be a little more adventurous when it comes to choosing food, darling.'

Darling! thought Emma scathingly. Well, that was definitely for the benefit of the waitress, not her. But why was Richard behaving like this? Was it simply good manners to avoid embarrassing other people by displaying the hostility between them? Or was there something more to it? She was relieved when the waitress returned with their drinks and she was able to take a sip of the bitter, refreshing liquid. In the background a western-style dance band began to play softly with a catchy rhythm and again that odd sense of unreality took hold of Emma. If it hadn't been for the tell-tale muscle twitching in Richard's cheek, she might have thought they were here for a second honeymoon. When the waitress returned to take their orders for the meal, the illusion was intensified. Letting his fingers close briefly over Emma's hand, Richard looked up at the waitress with the heart-stopping smile that had once made Emma go weak at the knees. Then he turned the smile back on Emma full force and she made the disturbing discovery that it still did make her go weak at the knees.

'I think some chicken satay with peanut sauce to begin with, don't you, sweetheart?' he suggested. 'And after that the rijstafel to share. And perhaps a platter of tropical fruit to follow. Oh, and please ask the drinks waiter to bring us a bottle of champagne.'

But when the waitress had glided away, Richard's smile vanished too. Leaning back in his chair, he drummed his fingers on the table in a rapid, staccato beat and scrutinised Emma's face with far less charm.

'I heard that Nigel Wellings went broke after he left you,' he announced.

Emma opened her mouth to protest that Nigel hadn't left her. In fact it had been the other way around. And then she wondered wearily what was the use. After all, she had grown used to Nigel's spite. He had been coldly furious when she had explained to him after a few months that she had mistaken her feelings, that she did not love him and never could. And on her father's death she had asked him to leave Prero's for good. He had never forgiven her and he had also told her in no uncertain terms that her money had been the only thing that had attracted him to her in the first place. Naturally that had hurt Emma's pride, but on the whole she had found it an enormous relief. Genuine love that ended was such a painful experience that she wouldn't wish it on anyone, even Nigel. And when he'd spread the rumours around Sydney that he had walked out on her, she had thought it more dignified not to protest. She thought it more dignified even now.

'Yes, I heard that too,' she said coolly, taking another sip of her drink. 'It was unfortunate for him.'

'Oh, I wouldn't say that,' said Richard in a danger-ously mild voice. 'In my opinion, it couldn't have happened to a more deserving man. But I suppose that if you were in love with him you may have felt differently about it.'

Emma flinched and said nothing, but fortunately the wine waiter arrived at that moment with their champagne and made a great fuss of uncorking and pouring it.

Still studying her face, Richard picked up his glass and smiled grimly as the man departed.

'Mind you, I did think you might come crawling back to me like a whipped puppy after he left you,' he announced in conversational tones. 'But I was surprised to find that you did have some pride, Emma.'

Emma had always had an explosive temper. Now, with her nerves ragged from the events of recent months, Richard's needling was simply too much.

'A puppy, Richard?' she mocked. 'Surely not. You're making a bad mistake if you think that I'm any kind of a lap-dog, *darling*. All you'll get from that theory will be a bite on the wrist.'

Richard swirled the champagne in his glass and looked at her over the rim. Then he took a sip and set it down.

'Oddly enough, that's quite a tempting prospect,' he said quietly. 'You still haven't lost your sexual allure, you know, Emma. As a matter of fact I still find you quite powerfully arousing.'

Emma caught her breath and stared at him in horror. Why did he have to say such things even if he thought them? And yet, although the tone of his voice was so dry that it robbed his words of any emotion, they still had a powerful impact. To her dismay she felt a shameful heat beginning to throb through her entire body. She bit her lip, terrified that she might make the equally outrageous statement that Richard hadn't lost his sexual allure either. Swallowing hard, she managed a small, cynical smile.

'You flatter me,' she said. 'But I find it hard to believe.'

'So do I,' agreed Richard grimly. 'After all, you're flat-chested, only passably pretty and your nose is too long. Added to that you've been spoiled rotten from birth, you have no conception of loyalty, you're extravagant, wilful and heartless. I just can't imagine why I should still find you attractive. But, oddly enough, I do.'

Emma's fury exploded like a supernova at these provocative words. Catching her breath, she stared back at him with glittering jungle-cat eyes.

'Really?' she challenged. 'Now you, on the other hand, are God's gift to women. Handsome, charming, rich, irresistibly sexy and possessing a wonderful way with words. I just can't imagine why I don't find you attractive. But, oddly enough, I don't!'

Richard's powerful brown hand came out and closed over her wrist.

'Don't mock me, Emma, or by heaven I'll make you regret it,' he said through his teeth.

'Stop making ridiculous threats, Richard!' she snapped. 'And come to the point. What is this proposition you want to discuss with me?'

'It's very simple, Emma. I propose to offer you a ninety-day bill, which will allow Prero's to keep trading for the next three months. In addition, I'll come to your rescue with that damned office block of yours. You need a tenant, I need new premises. Fielding's is expanding so rapidly we've outgrown our present quarters and I'm prepared to take over the lease you were offering Sawford's.'

A wave of shock and relief swept through Emma at this announcement. Her father's company need not go broke after all! She could still hold up her head and face the employees who depended on her for their livelihood.

Then seven years' experience of the cut and thrust of the business world settled on her like a damp, chill blanket of wariness.

'On what conditions?' she asked suspiciously.

Richard's lips drew back in a feral smile.

'Two,' he said softly. 'The first is that I am appointed managing director of Prero's immediately. With my expertise I believe that I can turn the business around and have it trading profitably by the end of three months. At that point you can resume control yourself if you wish.'

Emma's brain raced.

'And the second condition?' she asked, her throat constricting.

Richard paused before he replied. In the flickering candlelight, his eyes had a glitter that was almost menacing and his voice when he spoke was low and husky.

'That you come back to me as my wife—in the fullest sense of the word—during the three-month period in question.' He spoke as drily as if he were outlining a business clause. 'At the end of that time we can review the situation and make a final decision about our intentions. I imagine we'll get a divorce then.'

Emma almost swooned with shock at the outrageous implications of this suggestion.

'What do you mean?' she asked in a voice sharp with alarm. 'What do you mean "wife—in the fullest sense of the word"?'

Richard took another sip of champagne and smiled thinly.

'It's obvious, isn't it?' he demanded. 'I mean that we begin living together again. Sleeping together.'

He spoke the last two words with unmistakable relish.

Emma stared at him in disbelief.

'Why?' she burst out. 'You've just told me I'm spoilt, disloyal, extravagant, wilful and heartless!'

'All true,' agreed Richard. 'You left me for another man simply because of a stupid quarrel which wouldn't have made a blind bit of difference to any woman with an ounce of maturity or commitment. I've never forgiven you for that, Emma.'

'So what possible reason could you have for wanting to sleep with me now?' challenged Emma. 'You're not going to tell me it's love, are you?'

Richard's grip on her fingers tightened cruelly and his blue eyes glittered like chips of ice.

'Oh, no,' he murmured throatily. 'Not love, Emma. Revenge.'

CHAPTER TWO

EMMA was stunned that Richard could sit there smiling so blandly while uttering words that cut her to the heart. She swallowed hard, trying to contain her dismay. The silence between them lengthened. Plucking a frangipani flower out of the cut-glass bowl in the centre of the table, she crushed it unthinkingly in her fingers and inhaled its piercing sweetness. But before she could make any reply, the waitress arrived with the satay, creating a welcome diversion. Mechanically Emma put two of the little sticks with their juicy morsels of chicken on her plate and added a generous dollop of crunchy peanut sauce before giving the girl a strained smile. Yet when the waitress had departed she made no move to eat.

'Your food's getting cold,' Richard pointed out genially, as if his previous words had been nothing more harmful than a comment on the weather. 'Aren't you going to eat?'

She shook her head.

'Are you seriously going to sit there and tell me coldly that you want to sleep with me not out of love but just out of some power-crazed lust for revenge?' she blurted out at last.

'Yes.'

'Why?' she cried.

'Exactly for that reason,' replied Richard, swallowing a morsel of chicken and smiling at her. 'Power. I want to be in control of the situation for once instead of being some kind of bloody puppet for you and your father to manipulate.'

'You were never that!' exclaimed Emma indignantly.

'Wasn't I? Look, Emma, I married you because I fell in love with you and for no other reason, but right from the start your father tried to pretend I was after your money. And you were fool enough to believe him.'

'I didn't!' exclaimed Emma. 'I wouldn't have cared if you had had nothing. I left home and married you, didn't I? And lived in that horrid little house in Woolloomooloo?'

'And kept running back to Daddy every two minutes trying to kiss up to him,' retorted Richard scathingly.

'Only because I loved both of you. I wanted you to be friends. Is that so unreasonable?'

Richard gave a mirthless jeer of laughter.

'It was when you were dealing with someone like Frank Prero,' he retorted. 'He was determined to part us right from the start.'

'He wasn't! I know he didn't like the idea of our marriage at first, but he was coming around. Why do you think he gave you that big contract on the Manly shopping centre? Because he wanted to help you!'

Richard swore violently under his breath.

'Like hell he did! It was another one of his sneaky moves to separate us, Emma. I'm damned sure he was the one who made it impossible for me to get the materials I needed to complete the contract on time. Trying to put me out of business was his way of punishing me for daring to get involved with you.'

'Oh, it's easy to make rotten accusations against someone who is dead and can't defend himself,' she flared. 'But do you have any proof?'

'No, I don't,' he said through his teeth. 'But I'm sure of it all the same. Frank had a bad reputation in the dirty tricks department. But in any case, whatever your father had or hadn't done, if you'd been any kind of a wife you would have stuck by me in that crisis.'

'Oh, would I?' gasped Emma. 'Even when you stormed out of the house, insulting my father all the way, and didn't show your face for five days? And not only that but——'

'Listen, I don't pretend I was the perfect husband,' growled Richard, 'but I don't think my faults justify the kind of revenge you took. Any decent wife would have made allowances for the way I behaved that Christmas, instead of packing her bags and running home to Daddy.'

Emma's hand closed so hard around the stem of her wine glass that she almost snapped it. Gritting her teeth, she fought down the impulse to fling the contents in Richard's face. Oh, yes? she thought. Any decent wife would have just looked the other way while you had a squalid affair with another woman only eleven months after getting married, would she? Well, I couldn't do that. I hated you then, Richard, and I hate you now for the way you hurt me! But when she spoke, her words came out smooth and cold and brittle.

'Unfortunately I didn't happen to be a decent wife.'

Richard gave a sneering smile.

'Not then,' he agreed. 'But you have another chance now, sweetheart. This time round you can get it right. Come back to me and behave exactly the way I want you to.'

'Why?' demanded Emma in an unsteady voice. 'Why do you want me to do that?'

'I told you. I want to be in control of the relationship.'

'And if I refuse?'

Richard shrugged. 'Then you'll go broke.'

Emma let out her breath in a ragged sigh of disbelief.

'That's inhuman.'

'Any more inhuman than the way you treated me?'

Her hands would not be still. She picked up a satay stick and set it down again, fiddled with her knife, traced patterns on the tablecloth. And all the time a blinding misery like a tidal wave seemed to be building inside her. At last she could bear it no longer and she stared at him beseechingly.

'Richard, please! You said you married me because you loved me. If you have any of that feeling left towards me, don't torment me like this. It's cruel. It makes a mockery of what we once meant to each other.'

But Richard's face was so hard and pitiless, it might have been carved from granite.

'Ah, but I don't have any of that feeling left, Emma,' he said softly. 'Your own behaviour killed any love I had for you. All that's left is a certain reluctant but quite powerful physical attraction. I imagine three months or so of indulging that should burn it out pretty effectively.'

Emma closed her eyes briefly and shuddered.

'And then?'

'And then we can get a divorce. After all, I might want to marry someone else, someone I can love and respect.'

At these words she felt a jolt of horror as sickening as if she had just plunged ten floors in a lift. Her eyes flew open.

'Do you have someone in mind?' she demanded.

'Perhaps,' he said with an enigmatic shrug. 'Or for that matter you might want to marry again.'

Emma's face contorted into a stark smile.

'I don't think so. After what I've been through, I'm not wonderfully keen on marriage any more.'

Richard gave her a mocking smile and raised his glass of champagne.

'Then once I set your company in order you can dedicate your life to making money and having lovers, the things which you are wonderfully keen on. Can't you, darling?'

'You're such a swine, Richard,' she breathed.

'I'm glad you realise it, Emma. Well, what's your answer?'

Emma's entire body was shaking, but she tried to fight down her anger and think coolly and rationally. She had worked hard to build up the firm to the point where it was now, and if it hadn't been for the collapse of the Sawford bank she knew it would have been a prosperous business. Besides, there were people who worked for her, people who depended on her for their livelihood. What would happen to their jobs if she let the company go bankrupt? However much she hated Richard at this moment, loyalty to others urged her powerfully to accept his offer. But beneath that there was another reason: an insane, unwanted flare of longing to be in Richard's arms and in his bed again. It wasn't going to be permanent, she knew that, and it would probably bring her more pain than pleasure. But the sight of him had awoken all the old, clamorous physical need for him and perhaps the emotional need too. Even if she couldn't find love in his arms, maybe she could find a temporary quenching of the flames that scorched her. She bowed her head in bitter assent.

'It seems I have no choice.'

'Look at me, Emma. Tell me what you're going to do.'

Their eyes met—naked, burning with hatred and with something else.

'I'm going to come back to you as your wife,' she said through her teeth.

'Good,' murmured Richard as blandly as if she had just agreed to become his shorthand typist. 'Then I suggest you eat some of this excellent food and after that we'll go for a little stroll on the beach together before bed.'

Alarm bells rang noisily in Emma's head. She looked down at the chicken satay with as much horror as if it were deadly nightshade. In spite of the balmy, tropical air, her hands felt suddenly chill and clammy.

'Wh-when does this reunion begin?' she stammered.

Richard smiled lazily, his blue eyes narrowing with amusement.

'Oh, didn't I tell you? It begins tonight.'

Emma took a sudden gulp of champagne and choked.

'T-tonight?' she gasped, her eyes streaming.

'Yes. I stayed in another hotel in Sanur last night, but I've given orders for my luggage to be transferred to our bungalow this evening. It should be there by the time we get back from our walk.'

'I don't believe this,' she said, shaking her head in a dazed fashion. 'It's not really happening.'

'Yes, it is,' Richard assured her kindly. 'You'll find it much easier to believe tomorrow morning after...a good night's sleep. And don't worry. I'll send off faxes to my lawyers and my bank first thing after breakfast to organise the financial side of our agreement.'

Emma scarcely heard that last sentence. She was too busy panicking about the implications of 'a good night's sleep' in Richard's company. Trying hard to maintain an air of normality, she pulled one of the chicken pieces off its skewer, dipped it into the peanut sauce and ate it. To her surprise, she found it was delicious.

'The food is still very good here, isn't it?' she remarked, with the half-hysterical feeling that she was dreaming and would wake up at any moment.

This time Richard's smile seemed almost genuine.

'Yes. I've often thought about this place over the years and I suppose you have too or you wouldn't be here. Let me see, what else did we do last time we were here? Oh, yes. The trip to Penelokan. Now that really was a highlight. Perhaps we ought to set out tomorrow and see if it's still as beautiful as ever. What do you think?'

Emma stared at him as if he had gone insane. Was he really proposing to replay every detail of their honeymoon just as if the violent quarrels, the estrangement, the hostility of the last eight years had never existed? Well, if he was, perhaps the safest thing she could do was to humour him.

'That would be lovely, darling,' she said in a strained voice, looking wildly round the table for some means of escape. But all she could see was the waitress bearing down on them to remove their empty plates. Shortly afterwards the girl returned with the rijstafel—a fragrant and delectable array of pork, prawns, chicken, vegetable and curry dishes around a central mound of steamed rice. Richard helped Emma to a massive serving of everything and grimaced comically when he dropped a prawn in the centre of the flower arrangement.

'Oops, looks as if I'm still clumsy in the dining-room. Are you still as lousy at cooking as you used to be, Em?'

Emma pulled a face, torn between amusement and resentment.

'Not quite, but it isn't my favourite activity. I tend to buy a lot of take-aways and heat them in the microwave oven.'

'You cooked a chocolate cake once in the microwave oven. It rose and rose and then exploded. Do you remember?'

Her lips quirked involuntarily at the reminder.

'Yes, it was ghastly. I forgot the sugar, too. You ate it, though.'

'"Greater love hath no man",' he murmured.

A terrible sense of constriction gripped her chest as if a cold hand were squeezing her heart. How could he sit there and joke about it all, as if this reunion were genuine? As if the love which had carried them through those early trials of married life were still alive and burning brightly? She caught her breath and dropped her gaze.

'What's wrong?' he demanded.

'I wish you'd asked me to do anything else but this, Richard,' she replied in a passionate whisper. 'It's going to be so painful, so repellent. I can't bear it.'

The good humour died out of his face and his blue eyes were suddenly chill and merciless.

'You'll have to,' he said brutally.

They talked little during the remainder of the meal and even the luscious pineapple, cantaloup, mangoes and pawpaws which appeared as dessert failed to rouse Emma's enthusiasm. Her whole mind and body seemed to be focused on the single, alarming question—What's going to happen afterwards?

Yet when they finally finished their coffee and rode to the ground floor in the lift, Richard did not lead her straight back to the bungalow as she had half feared. Instead he put his arm around her shoulders and steered her towards the beach.

'Let's go and look at the ocean.'

The touch of his warm, muscular arm on her body made her flinch. She wanted so badly to relax into his embrace, to lean against his shoulder and rub her face against the light fabric of his jacket, to feel the beating of his heart. Instead she held herself stiffly aloof, trying to send out to him the silent message that, while she might have agreed to this farcical union, she was doing so under protest.

'I despise you for this,' she said unsteadily.

'Do you?' he retorted with a short laugh. 'Well, I think I can live with that. It really makes very little difference to me how you feel about it, Emma. It's how I feel that concerns me. And I feel quite satisfied.'

As the word 'satisfied' passed his lips, he brought her to a halt so suddenly that she was taken by surprise.

Hauling her savagely into his arms, he bent his head and kissed her. His body was hard and intoxicatingly virile against hers, with a wild spicy tang of cologne and masculine warmth that she found irresistibly arousing. He tasted of champagne and tropical fruit and, when his tongue slid between her lips, she offered no resistance. Instead, seized by some primitive instinct, she gave it a soft, teasing bite. His sharp intake of breath told her that that was a serious mistake and now his hard, merciless fingers began massaging her back in a sensual, urgent rhythm that she found wildly exciting. The eight lonely years without love vanished as if they had never existed. The world spun around her and suddenly she was a young woman on her honeymoon, tasting the delirious bliss of love in a setting that was made for romance.

Sighing sensually, she tilted her trembling lips to his and let her body sway in his hold so that she brushed lightly against him. The heated evidence of his arousal was unmistakable and he caught her by the hips, grinding himself against her so that she was in no doubt of what he wanted. She heard him give a low groan deep in the back of his throat, then he cupped her face in his hands and looked down at her so intently that she felt he was studying her. Overhead the palm fronds rustled lightly in the mild breeze and the tropical sky was like a dark blue banner ablaze with stars. An aching sweetness trickled through Emma's entire body as she met Richard's gaze and she felt herself quivering as if she were shaken by a fever. It wasn't too late for them, was it? Surely if Richard could still make her tremble and throb and yearn to cry out with this mysterious, molten passion there must be something between them worth saving? Mustn't there? It couldn't be mere lust that made him stare down at her so fiercely with that glittering moonlit gaze. Could it?

'Come on,' he said hoarsely. 'I can see you want this as badly as I do. I'd strip you off and have you here and now, Emma, down on that silver strip of sand with the foam surging around our bodies. But somebody else might come out for a walk. Better to be inside our house where you can let yourself go and moan and gasp and cry out when I take you, you beautiful, heartless little witch.'

Emma stiffened at that cruel taunt. Yes, it would be mere lust! Easily, very easily. In fact she would be a fool to deceive herself for one moment into thinking that Richard felt anything else for her. Wrenching herself out of his hold, she began walking furiously down the beach.

'Well, come on, then,' she said over her shoulder. 'What are you waiting for?'

Her gold evening shoes sank into the sand at every step and Richard had no difficulty at all in overtaking her. She almost hoped that he would ask for an explanation of her abrupt departure, so that she could tell him a few blistering home truths about himself. But he was too shrewd or too indifferent for that. He simply strode along beside her looking as relaxed and nonchalant as if they had come out for no other reason than to enjoy the soft hiss and rush of the waves breaking on the silvery sand, the sweet, potent fragrance of the tropical flowers and the moonlight shimmering over the water. Emma was seething so furiously that she almost missed the turn-off to their bungalow and Richard had to reach out and catch her hand.

'Let go of me!' she spat.

'Just as you like,' he replied in a soft, mocking voice. 'I can wait.'

When they reached the bungalow she hurried ahead of him, inserting her key into the door with shaking fingers and then rushing up the stairs and into the bathroom. Shutting the door behind her with a vicious slam, she leaned against it, her heart pounding.

'Damn him,' she muttered under her breath. 'Damn him, damn him, damn him!'

Her heavy, dark hair was falling out of its chignon and her make-up was smudged from Richard's kisses. A strange air of febrile excitement seemed to crackle dangerously about her as if she were a teenager who had just been kissed for the first time. It infuriated her to see herself looking so dishevelled in the mirror when she was used to being confronted by the image of a cool, composed businesswoman. With jerky, impatient movements, she took a pot of face cream out of her sponge bag and deliberately sponged every trace of make-up and of Richard off her face. Then she hauled off her clothes, flung them carelessly on the bathroom floor and stepped into the shower. It gave her a certain spiteful, childish pleasure to linger there. Let Richard wait if he wanted to use the bathroom! She hadn't invited him here, had she? Maybe he would take the hint and go somewhere else!

But at last the water began to run cold and she was forced to emerge. She rubbed herself dry and then stood there hesitating. What was she to do now? There had been no sound of a door closing below and she felt fairly certain that Richard was still out there, waiting for her. Her skin crawled with a half-delightful apprehension at the thought. Should she get dressed again? But the mere thought of climbing back into the same clothes made her grimace. Of course she could just wrap herself in a large bath-towel and go out like that. But it seemed like a terribly poor-spirited thing to do, especially when she was bound to have it ripped off her anyway. Well, she'd show Richard that she wasn't afraid of him! Defiantly she tossed back her long black hair, opened the bathroom door, and stepped out into the bedroom stark naked.

Richard had turned on the bedside lamps so that the room was bathed in a soft, apricot glow and he had taken off his dinner-jacket and shirt. At the sound of the opening door, he turned round and faced her and she felt an unwelcome pang of admiration at the sight of his lean, hard, muscular physique. The flare of interest in his eyes made her suspect that he was regarding her with a similar admiration. Her cheeks burned but she rested her hands defiantly on her hips.

'Well, is this what you want?' she demanded contemptuously.

'Yes.'

Without a trace of embarrassment, he strolled across the room, swept her up in his arms and planted a long, burning kiss on her mouth. Then, staring down at her with glittering blue eyes, he walked across to one of the huge beds and dropped her in the centre of it. Before she could utter more than a single indignant gasp of protest, he knelt astride her, pinioned her wrists on either side of her head and kissed her even more violently than before. Emma wanted to show her complete disdain for him by remaining totally unmoved and at first it was easy. She struggled angrily, turning aside her face from his kisses. But as his mouth travelled down the column of her neck in a series of soft, biting caresses she could not repress a faint moan of pleasure. He raised his head for a moment and she saw a flicker of triumph in his eyes. Then slowly, sensually he drew her nipple into his mouth and caressed it with his tongue. A tingle of pleasure so acute that it was close to pain flared through every nerve-ending in her body and she caught her breath and arched instinctively against him, writhing and shuddering under his touch. His lips released her, only to move further down her body, nibbling over her flesh in a provocative, rhythmic stimulation that drove her wild with longing. Her hands clenched tightly on the sheets and she closed her eyes, whimpering softly. When his mouth touched the most intimate, secret part of her, she started up with a shuddering gasp of protest of incoherent pleasure, but he thrust her back.

'Lie still and enjoy it,' he urged, his body so closely linked to hers that she could feel the vibration in his throat. She tried to remind herself that she hated him, that she was doing this only under protest, but her body seemed to have taken on a will of its own. And what it wanted it wanted urgently, violently, without any delay.

'Richard...we shouldn't...it's insane...'

'Yes, we should. And it isn't insane. I want this more than I've wanted anything in the past eight years and you do too. Don't you? Don't you? Admit it, Emma; tell me that you want me. Say it!'

He had hauled himself up in the bed and was looming above her now, supported on his forearms, with his half-naked body crushed against her. She could feel the warmth, the heat, the tension in that body, the unmistakable virile hardness of it, and she wanted him! Oh, how she wanted him! Not just to touch her and hold her and kiss her, wonderful as that was, but to plunge deep inside her until they were fused in a total union.

'Say it,' he rasped again.

'I want you, Richard,' she breathed.

'That's all I needed to know,' he said coldly.

And, to her astonishment and chagrin, he rose to his feet and stood staring down at her with a strange, ravenous mixture of desire and hatred in his eyes.

'Goodnight, Emma.'

She lay in shocked disbelief, instinctively drawing up the sheet to cover her nakedness, and watched as he swiftly finished undressing with his back turned to her, pulled on a pair of lightweight cotton pyjamas and climbed into the other bed. Then, without another word, he switched off the light and began breathing deeply and evenly. She didn't ask him why he was doing this. She already knew. It was an act of cold-hearted, calculating revenge. First the challenge had been to see whether he could excite her to the point where she actually wanted him and then, having demonstrated the humiliating fact that she did, he had twisted the knife by rejecting her. The bastard! The unutterable, manipulative bastard! She wanted to kill him...

Her heart was still pounding furiously and her body was hot and pulsing with the effects of unsatisfied desire so that it made her more angry than ever when a few minutes later she heard his quiet breathing deepen into the unmistakable rhythm of sleep. How could he lie there and just sleep when Emma herself wanted to cry and rage and throw things? It was inhuman! There must be some way she could get back at him for this, there must, there must! For hours she lay awake, tossing and turning, thumping her pillow and letting out occasional, low gasps of annoyance. But some time after three o'clock she fell asleep with her last conscious thought surging through her head as monotonously as the breaking surf outside. I hate him, I hate him, I hate him...

Her dreams were confused and anxious, centring not on the humiliating scene she had just endured but on the violent parting quarrel which had separated them eight years before, except that this time Richard didn't storm out without any explanation. Instead he came back to her and told her some long and complicated rigmarole which made everything magically all right. In the dream she was filled with a happiness so quiet and profound that it was like listening to lyrical music. Then the dream changed and she was in her office at Prero's, trying to make her father proud of her, feeling anxious and unhappy with a computer whirring in the background and the printer grinding. As she came slowly up to the surface of consciousness, she realised that it wasn't just a dream. There was a computer whirring right in this very room. Blinking, she sat up and squinted. It seemed quite crazy, but Richard was sitting at the fold-out mahogany desk in the corner of the room with a portable computer, the telephone and a tiny printer laid out in front of him. Without even stopping to think about how much she hated him, she spoke impulsively.

'What are you doing?'

He turned around and smiled at her, then tore a document off the printer and waved it in the air.

'Working. I'll have to get you to sign this in a moment. It's a faxed letter from my lawyer concerning our agreement about the office complex.'

His voice was neutral, even friendly. As the events of the previous evening came rushing back to her mind, Emma stared at him in consternation. Had she dreamt all those torrid details of what he had done to her? Her face flushed and she darted a quick, uneasy glance at him and then hastily looked away. No, she hadn't. That cruel, superior look of amusement around the edges of his lips made her certain that he remembered everything just as clearly as she did. Yet he chose not to refer to it. Why?

'Why don't you get dressed and we'll go and have breakfast on the balcony?' he suggested.

At a loss to know what else to do, Emma agreed.

'All right,' she said warily. 'Will you call Room Service and order it?'

'I already have.'

She was still naked and did not want to endure the embarrassment of climbing out of bed in front of that disconcertingly cool blue gaze. But even as she sat hesitating, with the sheet pulled up high in her armpits, Richard turned back to the computer as if he had already lost interest in her. Feeling rather affronted, Emma slid out of bed on the opposite side, groped in her suitcase for a dressing-gown and made her way to the bathroom. When she returned a few minutes later, dressed in a yellow cotton T-shirt, yellow and white daisy-patterned cotton skirt and casual sandals with her hair hanging loose, she found Richard already sitting at the table on the balcony with an array of iced juice, fresh tropical fruit, coffee and Danish pastries in front of him. Next to these was a camera, and a litter of guidebooks and maps. He smiled at her as if there had never been the slightest unpleasantness between them. The charm of that smile unnerved her.

' "Will you walk into my parlour?" said the spider to the fly,' she chanted under her breath.

'What did you say?' asked Richard, frowning.

'Nothing.'

'Sit down and eat,' he urged. 'Then we'll decide what we want to do with our holiday.'

The coffee was fragrant and full of flavour and the Danish pastries were unexpectedly crisp and delicious but Emma found it hard to keep her mind on her breakfast. All the time she was eating she kept darting Richard nervous, speculative glances, trying to figure out his intentions. Yet he seemed as cheerful and unruffled as if he really were just enjoying a long-awaited holiday. When at last her plate was empty, he slid one of the glossy coloured brochures across the table to her.

'Do you fancy an excursion to Penelokan?'

Emma flinched. His question brought a rush of unwelcome memories flooding back to her as she remembered the magical blue lake set high in the mountains in the northern part of the island. Lake Batur was located in the crater of a dormant volcano and the ascent to the nearby mountain and the few days they had spent exploring the idyllic countryside around it had been the highlight of Richard and Emma's honeymoon. For that very reason she now wanted to avoid it like a plague spot.

'No, I don't,' she said in a rush.

Richard shrugged indifferently.

'What would you like to do, then? After all, we still have quite a lot of time to kill in each other's company.'

That casual statement touched Emma on the raw. How could anybody speak of killing time in Bali, of all places? An idyllic tropical paradise whose magic had once enchanted her so thoroughly that she had believed every minute spent there was precious and irreplaceable. And of course she had once felt the same way about any time spent in Richard's company. Well, things had certainly changed! Her lips twisted into a cynical smile.

'I don't care what we do,' she retorted. 'Although frankly I hope we won't have to spend too much time alone together. Perhaps we could go to see some Balinese dancing, or go shopping, or do some local sightseeing.'

She tried to keep her voice as light and indifferent as his. There was no way she wanted Richard to guess her true reason for avoiding Penelokan—the fear that she would simply crack up and weep if she had to go there in his company. Besides, if she stayed here in the south of the island, she would still be close to the airport at Tuban. If she ever got too desperate, she could always flee back to Sydney.

But Richard didn't even seem to notice the faint tremor in her voice that marred her poise. He was leaning back in his chair with a mocking smile of triumph on his lips.

'All right,' he agreed lazily, picking up another pile of brochures and flicking through them. 'We'll do all those things. It'll be a second honeymoon, Emma.'

CHAPTER THREE

THEIR second honeymoon began that very morning with a swim in the nearby pool. It was another perfect, tropical morning. The sky overhead was blue and cloudless, the air was warm, moist and filled with the scent of flowers and the water in the swimming-pool sparkled invitingly. But Emma dawdled deliberately at the poolside, feeling reluctant to shed the protective cover of her thin green, cotton beach wrap. She didn't want Richard ogling her when she emerged in her bikini. Nor did she want to be lured into playing silly games in the water as if she were really enjoying his company. And his ostentatious concern for her comfort didn't make her feel any better disposed towards him. Even when he pulled up a cushioned banana lounge for her and or-dered a couple of iced fruit juices from a passing waiter, she didn't thank him but simply continued to glower at him. With a mocking smile, he took a swift gulp of his iced fruit juice, set down the glass and patted her pat-ronisingly on the head.

'Don't seethe too hard, darling,' he warned. 'You're raising the surrounding air temperature by at least five degrees, you know.'

Then, blowing her a kiss which only made her seethe even harder, he dived into the water. As she watched him cleaving up the blue pool in a powerful, surging freestyle, her simmering resentment was quenched for a moment by an unwilling spurt of admiration. At the age of thirty-five, Richard still had a magnificent body—powerful, muscular, honed by years of hard, physical

labour, it carried not an ounce of spare fat. His skin
was tanned honey-gold by exposure to the sun and his
fair hair was still thick and curly. If she hadn't disliked
him so much, she would have felt a throb of primitive
desire at the sight of him almost naked in the clear, still
waters of the pool. As it was, she tore her gaze away
from him to the other occupants of the area and recognised the honeymoon couple who had been on the bus
the previous day. They were disporting themselves joyfully with all the carefree abandon of youth, duck-diving,
tickling each other, playing complicated games and frol-
icking together like exuberant dolphins. As she watched,
the young man suddenly surged up out of the water with
his wife giggling and shrieking on his shoulders. Then,
with a growl of mischievous laughter, he sent her deliberately catapulting forward into the water. While she was
still gasping and threshing and uttering laughing cries of
complaint, he swam swiftly across to the poolside,
reached out his hand to one of the glasses of iced fruit
juice and took a long gulp.

'Oh!' cried Emma in belated warning. 'Wait a minute.
That one belongs to my husband!'

The young man flashed her a rueful grin and his brown
eyes twinkled disarmingly.

'Oh, hell, does it?' he demanded. 'Look, I'm awfully
sorry. We had a couple of drinks just like those somewhere along the side. Yes, there they are down by that
stone elephant. I'll tell you what, let me buy your
husband another one.'

He hauled himself out of the water and called to a
passing waiter. Richard and the young woman in the
water, attracted by the commotion, both swam over to
the side to find out what was going on. There was a
hasty babble of explanations.

'Don't worry about it,' urged Richard, emerging from
the water and picking up a towel. But by then the waiter

had already returned with a fresh glass of juice. 'Put it on my account,' insisted Richard, waving away the young man's protests. 'Bungalow number five. Fielding.'

'Yes, sir.'

'Thanks very much,' said the embarrassed young man. 'I feel a real fool about this.'

'Don't let it worry you,' said Richard. 'Look, why don't you both come and have a drink with us?'

Emma averted her eyes as Richard hastily towelled his wet body and pulled on a beach robe. But the newlyweds didn't bother with such formalities. Still making calf-eyes at each other, they pulled up a couple of bamboo lounges and sat down in their wet swimsuits.

'I'm Steven Castle and this is my wife Julie,' said the young man, stumbling slightly over the word 'wife'.

Julie blushed.

'Richard and Emma Fielding,' replied Richard, shaking hands.

'We're on our honeymoon,' explained Julie rather unnecessarily as she turned a smouldering glance on her brand-new husband.

'So are we,' replied Richard, turning an equally smouldering glance on Emma. 'Our second one, that is. We spent the first one here in Bali too.'

'Oh, really?' sighed Julie. 'How romantic! And you liked it so much that you came back? That's great!'

'Yes, great,' said Emma, giving Julie a small, tight smile and flashing Richard a glare that would have melted a polar ice cap.

But Julie wasn't easily discouraged.

'How long ago was the first one?' she demanded conversationally, simultaneously sipping her drink and sliding one arm through Steven's.

'Nine years ago,' said Richard.

Julie's face took on a radiant, wistful look.

'So I suppose you have kids back home now?' she suggested.

Richard's blue eyes flicked over Emma with an unreadable expression. Then he smiled urbanely at Julie and raised his glass.

'No, I'm afraid we haven't been blessed with children yet, much as I'd like to have them. And I'm sure Emma would too.'

Even the exuberant Julie was a little disconcerted by this but she quickly recovered.

'Well, you'll just have to keep trying, then, won't you?' she said. 'And what better setting could you have for it than this? I think it's the most romantic place in the world.'

'Julie,' muttered her husband, giving her a quiet nudge and jerking his head at Emma's stony features. 'I think we ought to go and take a shower before lunch. Excuse us, won't you? And thanks for the drink.'

'Why on earth did you say a thing like that?' burst out Emma once the couple were out of earshot and the poolside was deserted again.

'Like what?'

Richard had stripped off his beach robe and was lying back on the banana lounge with his muscular arms stretched up behind his head as lazily as if he had nothing on his mind but enjoying the sunshine.

'All that rubbish about wanting children,' retorted Emma.

He raised one tawny eyebrow reprovingly.

'I do want children,' he said.

For a moment Emma was taken aback. A strange thrill of excitement went through her, followed immediately by intense suspicion.

'Oh, yes,' she said sarcastically. 'With me, I suppose?'

Richard sighed and shook his head.

'No. When I eventually do have children, I want to feel sure that they're mine.'

She flushed scarlet at the implicit insult.

'You swine,' she said. 'Are you implying that you wouldn't feel sure, if I were their mother?'

'If the cap fits...' murmured Richard provocatively.

'Are you calling me promiscuous?' demanded Emma.

This time the provocative note in his voice was unmistakable.

'If I am, you only have your own behaviour to blame for it,' he drawled. 'You were pretty quick off the mark with good old Nigel, weren't you? And there have been others since then.'

Emma gritted her teeth. In fact, there hadn't been anyone except in the over-fertile mind of journalists. It was also outrageously unfair. Her face took on a haunted look as she remembered how it had happened. If she hadn't been so agonisingly hurt over the discovery of Richard's infidelity, she doubted whether she would ever have looked twice at the chief marketing manager of Prero's. In normal circumstances Nigel's rather glossy charm and showy lifestyle would have repelled her. But those hadn't been normal circumstances. Twenty years old and deeply wounded, she had still decided to give Richard another chance. Her face contorted as she remembered that long begging letter she had written to him and entrusted to her father to deliver by hand. There hadn't been a word of reply from Richard, not a word! Alone on her first wedding anniversary, Emma had been easy prey when Nigel had arrived on the scene with a bottle of wine and a lot of glib sympathy. Yet it hadn't taken her long to work out that her involvement with him was prompted not by love but by a defiant attempt at revenge on Richard. Horrified at her own behaviour, she had soon broken it off, without having slept with him. But what right did that give Richard to criticise?

After all, he was the one who had betrayed her first and she had better grounds than the glossy tabloids for knowing that he had had numerous affairs since then.

'I think you're being very unfair!' she burst out. 'Haven't you heard of Women's Lib, Richard? You've been involved with other women while you were still married to me, haven't you?'

'True,' he admitted blandly.

'Then why shouldn't I get involved with other men?'

'Nobody's trying to stop you, sweetheart,' he replied in a dangerously silky voice. 'I'm simply making the point that I would like to have children soon and you're a totally unsuitable candidate to be their mother.'

Emma took a quick, shuddering breath and clenched her fists. There was no way she wanted to be the mother of Richard's children, although once the thought would have filled her with unbearable happiness, but his gibe still infuriated her. Her yellow-flecked green eyes flashed sparks.

'So what do you intend to do?' she demanded.

He squinted into the sun, and then adjusted a nearby beach umbrella so that it cast a cooling shadow over him.

'I'll probably get a divorce and marry someone else once this little interlude with you is over,' he replied.

Emma stared at him in dismay, remembering his cryptic hint the previous evening that he just might have her successor already picked out.

'Do you have someone special in mind?' she asked sharply.

'Very special,' he replied with a secretive smile.

The hide of it took her breath away. How could he just sit there, as good as telling her that he was in love with some other woman and that he still intended to sleep with her out of some crazy idea of revenge? It was outrageous, unforgivable!

'You——' She broke off. 'Then why are you here with me?'

'I've told you, Emma,' he replied, his blue eyes glinting. 'You've been a sort of minor obsession of mine lately. In fact, you're rather like a case of psoriasis. Easy to diagnose, but hard to get rid of.'

'Thanks! All my life I've wanted a man to compare me to a skin disease.'

'You're welcome. But the comparison is more accurate than you know. I've had a lot of trouble with the itch, the flare-ups, the impossibility of putting my mind to anything else while I'm still suffering from it. So I decided the best way to cure it was probably to indulge it.'

'Wonderful,' retorted Emma. 'And what choice do I get in the matter?'

'You've had your choice. And your payment. Prero's, in exchange for your body.'

'You really think anything can be bought, don't you?' she blazed.

'Certainly. It's a lesson I learnt from you and your father.'

With a gasp of indignation, Emma fell to her knees beside him and slapped his face soundly. The red imprint of her fingers appeared on his cheek, but he scarcely seemed to notice it. Seizing her right hand, he held it in a grip that hurt.

'Uh-uh,' he said softly. 'No violence. That's not part of the game.'

'It isn't a game!' she choked.

'Oh, yes, it is.'

'Then get it over with!' she exclaimed, her breath coming in unsteady gulps. 'Come to bed with me now and then release me from this ridiculous, humiliating situation.'

He was holding both her hands now and his grip had become soft and caressing. His thumbs stroked lightly over the backs of her hands, sending a tingling feeling of need coursing through her entire body.

'It's gratifying to hear you beg, Emma,' he murmured. 'And I can assure you that eventually I will come to bed with you. But it will be when and as I choose. In the meantime, I think we should do a little sightseeing, don't you? What do you say to a look round the stone-carvers' workshops at Batubulan today?'

Emma said only one thing.

'Go to hell!'

Emma stared sightlessly out of the car window as it bowled along the Klungkung road towards Batubulan. Normally she would have been fascinated by the unfamiliar sights skimming past outside. Lush, tropical forest and vivid green farmland interspersed by housing compounds with thatched pagodas rising towards the sky slowly gave way to Denpasar, the capital, with its pungent drains, noisy market-place and brightly coloured horse-drawn carriages decorated with bells. All the misery of the East, she thought bitterly, and I simply can't enjoy it because I'm far too preoccupied with a much bigger mystery—namely, what on earth am I doing here with Richard? She stole a swift, furtive glance at her husband and felt herself blush hotly as his gaze met hers. He frowned and immediately turned back to the road, while Emma dug her nails into her palms and wished she could emigrate to Mars.

It was a ridiculous, impossible situation in which to find herself. Married and yet not married. On a honeymoon and not on a honeymoon. Closer together than they had ever been in the past eight years and yet so far apart that you could fire a machine gun between them and not hit anyone. The worst of it was that, while

Richard seemed physically unchanged from the twenty-six-year-old man she had married, emotionally he was a total stranger to her now. Oh, he had always been ambitious. From the moment she had first met him, when he was only a sunburnt, hardworking builder of very few words, she had sensed immediately that he had hidden depths. It had come as no surprise to her to learn that he was studying law part-time and, when he'd confided in her that he intended to make Fielding Constructions the biggest building firm in Sydney, she had never doubted his ability to do it. He had always been so dynamic, so certain of his own abilities, so committed to throwing himself heart and soul into anything he did. It was no wonder that he had succeeded so spectacularly. The degree in law, the huge real-estate holdings, the mansion in Vaucluse. Emma felt a hollow sense of regret that she hadn't been able to share those triumphs with him. And she felt an even worse sense of regret at the savage and total destruction of the love that had once existed between them. For today Richard was no longer the passionate, explosive-tempered, generous, warmhearted man she had married. Instead he had become a cold, cynical, vindictive stranger who was prepared to use her and discard her like a bought woman because she had once dared to look at another man.

A dry, painful sob rose in her throat, but she turned it hastily into a cough and stared out of the car window. Yet it was impossible to turn her back on her own mounting sense of agitation. What Richard was demanding from her was cruel and inhuman. And the fact that she was still legally married to him, still loved him, made it worse, not better. Still love him? her brain echoed in horror. Of course you don't still love him! But, even as her mind leapt into a dazzling, gymnastic sequence of denials, her uneven heartbeat and the aching sense of nostalgia deep inside her were giving her a different message. She glanced sideways at that stern, disapproving profile and a painful, searing insight blazed through her so that she caught her breath. No, it was better to be honest with herself. She did love Richard and probably always would. In spite of the fact that he had betrayed her with another woman. In spite of the way he was taking such cruel revenge for her own frailties.

The realisation appalled her. If she could have hardened her heart and smiled cynically at Richard's demands, she might have come out of this situation quite unscathed. As it was, she was completely at his mercy and bound to be very badly hurt. She winced at the thought.

'Will you stop it?' he snarled.

'Stop what?'

'Sighing and moaning, and pulling faces as if somebody has just died!'

'I feel as if somebody has just died.'

'Well, I'm sorry that the prospect of going to bed with me fills you with such unmitigated rapture, sweetheart! But a deal is a deal. Sobbing into your sarong is not going to let you off the hook.'

'I didn't suppose it was, with your charming self in control of the situation!' she replied sweetly.

'God Almighty!' roared Richard. 'Sometimes I could wring your neck, Emma!'

'The feeling's mutual,' she snapped.

Exhilaration sang in her veins. For one crazy moment she felt almost as if they were in one of those shouting matches that had been so frequent in their brief married life. Crackling quarrels that had flared into action like bush fires and eventually been extinguished in bed, smothered beneath a torment of kisses, sighs, passionate embraces and creaking bed-springs. A wave of nostalgia swept over her, then her face suddenly looked cold and shuttered. Their present problems would never be as easy to solve as those meaningless tiffs...

Richard glanced at her sharply, then looked back at the road with stormy blue eyes and jutting jaw.

'I'm not planning on raping you, you know,' he growled. 'Anything that happens between us will happen only with your consent.'

'Really?' said Emma, although her throat was aching so badly she could hardly force out the words. 'Then what are you planning?'

His hand came over on to her knee, deftly twitching away at the thin folds of the sarong she was wearing. Then his warm fingers trickled teasingly up the smooth inner flesh of her thigh. She shuddered, consciously willing herself not to shift sensually, inviting his caresses. Only the tell-tale muscle in his cheek made her suspect that he was as hotly and powerfully aroused as she was herself by the gesture. But he covered her legs again and withdrew his hand lazily to the steering-wheel.

'I'm planning to enjoy you fully whenever I choose to do so,' he replied brutally. 'Provided of course that I can trust you to keep the terms of the agreement.'

She gave a raw croak of laughter.

'Oh, you can trust me. You've bought my co-operation by giving me Prero's. Haven't you?'

'Exactly,' he agreed in a steely voice. 'But there's no need for either of us to be ungracious about it, Emma. Why shouldn't we enjoy ourselves touring around Bali?'

'Enjoy ourselves?' she said incredulously. 'You might just as well ask me why we shouldn't enjoy ourselves walking on hot coals!'

'Some people do, I believe,' he remarked. 'In Fiji, at any rate.'

'Well, I'm not Fijian!'

'A pity. I'd like to see you walk across fire for me, Emma.'

'I'll bet you would. But it's not going to happen.'

He didn't pursue the matter, but drove on in silence until they reached the leafy village of Batubulan, which was the centre of the island's stone-carving. Parking the car in a shady, off-road patch of lush grass, Richard came round and opened the door for her. Frostily she ignored his helping hand as she climbed out, but her antagonism failed to provoke him.

'I need some garden statues for my new home in Vaucluse,' he remarked. 'I thought you might like to help me choose them and perhaps a few stone benches as well. Are you still fond of gardening, Emma?'

'Not really. I haven't time,' she replied.

'A pity. You really made our little balcony in Woolloomooloo into something special.'

She winced at the reminder. Haphazard cook, pyromaniac ironer and relentless producer of pink underwear, she had at least had one home-making skill, however useless: green fingers. It touched her that Richard even remembered after all this time but it also hurt her to the quick. Wasn't it absurd for them still to be legally married and yet to know so little about each other's lives? She didn't even know the name of this mysterious girl-friend whom Richard might or might not be planning to marry. Wouldn't it be better if Emma gave up the pretence that things were ever going to come right between them and filed for a divorce, as soon as possible? But a feeling of desolation swept over her at the thought and her face shadowed.

'What's wrong?' asked Richard.

'I was just thinking that we should get a divorce,' she replied heavily.

Once inside the building she was conscious of his eyes following her as she roamed about looking at the half-finished statues. The air was stiflingly hot, choking with dust and ringing with the noise of the workmen's hammers, so she was rather relieved when a small man in a brown sarong, beige shirt and yellow headscarf approached them.

'Can I help you, sir?'

'My wife and I would like to see some garden statues and benches.'

He led them into a leafy yard enclosed by the inevitable carved stone walls and ringed with dusty hibiscus bushes. Here a positive army of statues was displayed. Bulging-eyed monsters with long fangs, drooping tongues and curly beards stood side by side with serene-faced Buddhas and exuberant floral wall panels. Emma strolled among them with a reluctant feeling of interest. Wouldn't it be nice if she and Richard really were planning a garden to use for the rest of their lives? A garden where these boisterous stone warriors would remind them of happy times shared on an exotic little island just below the equator. You fool, she told herself.

'What would you like, Emma?'

'I don't care. I'm not likely to be seeing it for very long anyway. You choose.'

Frowning slightly, he pointed out several statues and garden benches, along with some panelled wall carvings, and then walked into the office with the proprietor to organise payment and shipping. Left alone, Emma ran her hand over one of the mossy, crumbling stone walls and sighed. She was beginning to feel horribly surly and ungracious and the feeling worried her. Although Richard had driven her into a corner so skilfully that she could hardly help being surly, it didn't suit her temperament. Even the strain and worry of business pressures had never set her nerves so badly on edge. Besides, she liked to be on friendly terms with everyone she met. Belatedly she wondered if she had hurt the stone-carver's feelings by her indifferent response to his work. With a twinge of guilt, she hurried into the office, where the deal was just being completed.

'Thank you very much for the statues,' she said, smiling warmly at the workman. 'They're really beautiful. I'll be so happy to have them in my garden.'

'*Kambali*,' replied the man. 'It's a pleasure.'

Richard gave her a rather surprised, scrutinising look as they returned to the car, but he did not mention her change of attitude. Instead he made an oblique suggestion.

'Do you think you'd enjoy having dinner over at Kuta Beach tonight?' he asked. 'Then we could come back to Bona after sunset and watch some of the dancing.'

'All right,' agreed Emma warily. 'That would be nice.'

Unexpectedly, it was nice. They reached the west coast of the island in time to watch the sun set at Tanah Lot. It was an enchanted place where a small temple sat perched on a rocky island about a hundred metres out from the coast. The fiery ball of the sun was just on the point of sinking into the blazing ocean as they arrived and against the vast red glowing backdrop of the sky and the sea the temple pagodas stood out as dark and sharp as the silhouettes of Norway spruce trees. Close in to the shore, the waves boiled and sucked against the rocks and flung themselves on the beach with a loud, crashing roar. Yet Emma and Richard did not have long to enjoy the view. Within moments of leaving their car, they were surrounded by a throng of shrill-voiced, determined little business people. Bright-eyed little girls with missing front teeth and enchanting smiles clutched at Emma's sarong while brandishing their wares in their free hand. Boys scarcely any older delivered a smooth salesman's patter in English and Bahasa Indonesia as they juggled their wares like conjurors.

'You like to buy, you like to buy?'

Within moments, Emma, who was too soft-hearted to resist, was totally engulfed. Two dress lengths of brilliantly coloured cloth, one scarlet, one gold, with silver floral patterns imprinted on them, were wound around her shoulders. A dancer's head-dress in imitation gold with tiny mirrors sat insecurely on her head, and her arms were full of ornate, carved boxes, bone carvings and filigree wooden fans threaded with red and yellow ribbon. Richard burst out laughing as he produced his wallet and paid for all this.

'I'd better get you out of here while you can still walk!' he exclaimed. 'No, no more, thank you, kids. It's really great stuff, but we've got enough now!'

Taking one of the dress lengths from Emma's shoulders, he opened it up to form an impromptu bag.

'Put the stuff in here and I'll carry it for you, otherwise you'll lose half of it.'

She obeyed, casting him a thoughtful sideways look. It surprised and perturbed her to see Richard entering so whole-heartedly into the spirit of the bazaar. When they reached the car, and he stowed her purchases safely away in the boot, she smiled uncertainly at him.

'You didn't have to pay for all that,' she said. 'I had some Indonesian money with me. Besides, I always thought you hated it when I bought things I didn't really need.'

'Don't be silly,' said Richard sharply.

He opened the car door for her and chased off the last remnants of giggling, squealing children by pulling fearsome faces and making demon noises at them. Then he climbed in the other side of the car.

'You talk about me as if I'm some kind of ogre, Emma.'

'I'm sorry, I didn't mean——'

'I know. I know what you meant. But don't go by what I was like nine years ago. I had a lot of business debts then that were worrying me and I wanted to make sure that our future together would be secure as possible. I never intended to spoil any of your harmless pleasure in having nice things. I'm sorry if I did.'

'It doesn't matter now,' said Emma in a subdued voice.

But it did. Like everything else in their marriage, it seemed to have a ripple effect that was still spreading out years afterwards, making waves. She pressed her fingers to her forehead and sighed. She had been terribly extravagant when they were first married, she realised that now. She'd been brought up as an adored only child, and it had never occurred to her not to just go out and buy anything she wanted; it had also never occurred to her that perhaps Richard couldn't afford the things she bought.

'I'm sorry too,' she said. 'I didn't have a clue about money then. I must have made things very difficult for you.'

He gave her a strange look.

'At the time I thought you were worth the difficulty,' he said.

They didn't speak again until they reached Kuta Beach and then their conversation was only about food.

'What kind of meal would you like to eat?' asked Richard. 'Japanese? Mexican? German? Chinese?'

Emma let out an explosive giggle.

'I thought we were supposed to be in Indonesia!' she cried.

'We are, but you wouldn't know it at Kuta. Come on, what's it to be?'

'Um, Swiss!' cried Emma, making the most unlikely choice she could think of.

Within half an hour they were cosily tucked up in a carved wooden booth, devouring *Bratwurst*, *Kartoffel-salat* and vast plates of *Apfelstrudel* while a cassette in the background provided energetic bursts of Swiss yodeling. Unexpectedly it was a lot of fun and Emma was surprised to find herself relaxing and even smiling when she caught Richard's eye.

'Goodness!' she said as their coffee with cream arrived. 'It makes me feel quite homesick.'

'That's right. You went to a Swiss boarding-school, didn't you?' demanded Richard.

She nodded.

'Did you like it? You never told me much about it.'

'Well, I was desperately homesick at first. I begged Dad not to send me but he wouldn't listen. I was only twelve and I hated the thought of being so far away from everyone I loved.'

'Everyone you loved?' said Richard in an odd voice. 'Who do you mean by that?'

Emma shifted awkwardly and spread her hands.

'Oh, you know. Dad.' She bit her lip. 'I suppose that's all, really. There wasn't anyone else unless you count Miss Matty.'

'No, there wasn't anyone else,' repeated Richard in a voice full of meaning. 'And that was the way your father wanted to keep it, wasn't it? I'll bet that's why he sent you off to boarding-school on the other side of the world, Emma. So that even if you did manage to make friends you wouldn't be able to keep them once you'd left there. He wanted you all to himself like a little princess shut up in a tower.'

'That's ridiculous!' protested Emma.

'Is it?' challenged Richard. 'You know, when I first met you, Emma, I couldn't get over what a lonely, sheltered existence you were leading. No job, no friends, nothing except that great barrack of a house and only your father for company whenever he could spare the time from his business affairs. It was a completely unnatural existence for a young girl. I felt really sorry for you.'

'Oh, is that why you married me?' asked Emma. 'Because you were sorry for me?'

'In a way,' agreed Richard, looking down into his glass and sighing heavily. 'I certainly wouldn't have married you then if I hadn't thought that things were seriously wrong with your home life.'

Emma felt as if someone had punched her in the stomach. She had always believed that Richard had married her because he loved her, even if things had gone horribly wrong later on. Was he telling her now that it was only pity?

'Thanks a lot,' she retorted. 'It was really kind of you to take pity on me.'

He caught her by the wrist.

'Don't be ridiculous, Emma,' he said. 'There was a lot more to it than that. You know damn well I didn't just marry you out of pity. I married you because I loved you. But if things had been different between you and your father I wouldn't have been in such a hurry to do it. For God's sake, you were only nineteen at the time. You should have had longer to become sure of your own feelings towards me, to get to know other men. And maybe it was selfish of me to go ahead with it when I did, but I could see too damned clearly what would happen if I didn't. Your father would keep you under his thumb so effectively that you'd never have a chance to make a real choice of your own again. You'd wind up just marrying whoever he picked out for you and that would probably be some money-grubbing bastard who didn't care a damn about you. Someone just like your father.'

Emma stared at him as a rapid hail of emotions tore through her like bullets—first an instinctive relief at the assurance that Richard had loved her, followed at once by rage and dismay at his attack on her father. The conflict of these responses made her feel deeply hurt and confused.

'You're being totally unfair!' she protested. 'I wasn't under my father's thumb and anyway he loved me.'

'In his own, twisted way perhaps,' agreed Richard grimly. 'I don't think anyone else would call it love, though. What it was all about was power, Emma—controlling every detail of your life, treating you like a wind-up doll that he could direct. And he wanted that control to extend not only to the school you went to, the friends you made, the clothes you wore, the job you did or didn't do, but even to the man you married.'

'Don't be ridiculous!' exclaimed Emma. 'Dad would never have tried to tell me who to marry!'

Then she hesitated. Wouldn't he? Hadn't he tried very hard to push Nigel Wellings on her? And hadn't he been furious when she'd first announced her marriage to Richard? But no, it was ridiculous!

'Yes, he would,' insisted Richard. 'He was seething when you married me and you know it.'

'Only because he thought you were after my money. He was coming round later.'

'He wasn't. That was part of his low cunning and we both got sucked in by it, Emma. He only pretended to like me so he could destroy me more easily.'

'That's not true,' insisted Emma. 'Even after you walked out on me, he wanted things to come right between us. He did everything he could to make it happen.'

'Oh, did he?' sneered Richard. 'I can't say I noticed.'

Emma thought bitterly of the letter she had entrusted to her father, the letter begging Richard to come back to her to sort out their differences. A barb of pain went through her at the memory.

'Oh, what does it matter now?' she demanded. 'My father's dead and gone. And our marriage is on the rocks, Richard, and has been for years. You won't change anything by raking over the past. Anyway, if we're going to this dancing, hadn't we better leave now?'

The Kecak dance was already in progress when they reached Bona and they had to stumble through semi-darkness to reach their seats overlooking the dance area. The central performance area was lit only by a large, flaming lamp and in its flickering red lights the dancers' moving forms cast huge, threatening shadows. There was no accompanying orchestra. Instead a chorus of men, dressed only in black and white checked sarongs with a red flower behind their right ear and a white one behind their left, moved in a circle, uttering a strange, hypnotic cry.

'Chak! Chak! Chak!'

Emma had only a vague notion of the story behind the dance, but knew it was about the virtuous wife Sita who was kidnapped by a demon king and torn away from her beloved husband's side. Yet, however little Emma understood the fine detail, she felt a glow of relief when the young lovers were reunited at the end. If only real-life problems could have such simple, satisfying solutions!

'It was breathtaking, wasn't it?' she exclaimed, turning to Richard as the performance ended. 'But why was her husband so furious with her early on in the piece?'

Before he could reply, the dancers came on to take a bow, Sita looking demure in a head-dress smothered in white frangipani blooms, a heavily embroidered top, and a green sarong with yellow sash, while Rama beside her looked every inch the aggrieved but triumphant husband. But as the lights around the edge of the courtyard came on and they filed out of their places, Richard's powerful fingers gripped her arm and he answered her question.

'Because he felt he could never forgive her for being unfaithful to him,' he murmured. 'And who could blame him? It's the one form of treachery no red-blooded man could ever pardon. I know I never could.'

CHAPTER FOUR

FOR the next few days there was an uneasy truce between Emma and Richard. Emma felt as if she was walking on very thin ice and she had no desire whatsoever to plunge into the freezing depths below, so her solution was simply to back away. In the daytime, especially in the company of other people, she behaved as if she and Richard really were on a honeymoon. Light, friendly conversation, a readiness to accompany him on short excursions, a smiling, relaxed air as if she were having a good time. At night and in private it was a different matter. Every footfall, every sudden, unexpected look made her start nervously. For she was still half dreading, half yearning for the moment when Richard would exact the final completion of their bargain. All the same, she was quite unprepared for his blunt announcement three days before the end of their holiday. They had just finished eating breakfast on their balcony, when he rose to his feet with a purposeful look.

'You'd better pack a few clothes in an overnight bag,' he told her. 'I want to go to Penelokan and I think it's a waste of time trying to do it all in one day.'

'Penelokan?' she echoed, appalled. 'Why?'

'Because it's a beautiful place and it's a shame to leave Bali without seeing it again. Come on, let's get moving before the weather gets too hot.'

It was a distance of probably no more than seventy kilometres from Sanur, but the journey took them over two hours. Balinese roads seemed to be thronged with every imaginable vehicle and pedestrian from horse-

66

drawn carriages to strong-minded ducks, all of which operated by highly independent traffic codes. Richard was kept quite busy honking the horn, slowing to a snail's pace and weaving patiently around old ladies with bundles on their heads who thought the middle of the main road was just the place for a good gossip. At least this left Emma free to think, but her thoughts brought her no comfort. She didn't want to go to Penelokan with Richard. The place was too deeply imbued with memories which should have been precious, but were now unbearably painful.

Her cheeks grew hot at the mere thought of how they had climbed Mount Batur together on their honeymoon and stood on the rim of its steaming crater vowing undying love for each other. Even worse was the memory of the passionate encounter in their bedroom at Air Panas that night. Not to mention that final moment when they had stopped at Penelokan for a last glimpse of the lake before returning home. Richard, tough, unsentimental Richard, had hauled her into his arms and kissed her violently on the mouth. And then he had spoken words she had thought she would cherish for the rest of her life. 'Emma Fielding, I swear I'll love you until that mountain is levelled and that lake runs dry.'

Her lips twisted bitterly now at the memory. What a joke it was! But why did Richard want to drag her back there? Was it some cruel streak of sadistic humour that prompted this expedition? Was he determined to punish and humiliate her by callously using her body in a place where they had once been so happy? There seemed no other possible explanation.

As the car climbed into the hills, the warm, damp blanket of air outside seemed to grow lighter and cooler. When they stopped to stretch their legs ten kilometres from Lake Batur the atmosphere was fresh and invigorating. The hotel staff had given them a packet of chicken sandwiches, a basket of tropical fruit and cold drinks so that they were able to have a picnic by the roadside. Leafy thickets of bamboo rustled in the breeze, sending dancing shadows over the long green grass. A carved Buddha sat cross-legged in one of the countless wayside shrines, his stone niche so overgrown with moss and ferns that he seemed in danger of being swallowed at any moment by the jungle. Somewhere there was the sound of running water and then overhead a sudden flutter of sound. A curious, chiming noise like the tinkling of distant bells. Emma glanced sharply up.

'How odd!' she exclaimed. 'For a moment I thought I heard bells.'

'You did,' agreed Richard with a smile. 'It's a Balinese bird orchestra. The local people hang bells and little flutes around the necks of doves so that they can hear the music when they fly.'

'Goodness,' said Emma. 'What an odd, beautiful idea! But where did you find out about it, Richard? I didn't remember hearing it last time we were here.'

He gave her a strange look. Long, hard, penetrating.

'No, we didn't. But I've been coming back to Bali once a year since then.'

She felt shocked and somehow violated, as if he had just told her that he had been breaking into her house and searching it once a year. For some unfathomable reason she had felt that their past was safely locked up, untouchable. And for her the memories of Bali were so closely linked with Richard that she could never have borne the pain of returning alone year after year merely for carefree holidays. So why had Richard come? Was it because he was too insensitive to remember her at all? Or…her breath began to come in fast, uneven gulps…or was it a kind of pilgrimage? Were the memories of their time together too precious for Richard to give them up?

Suddenly she felt she had to know. Yet embarrassment made her voice come out unnaturally shrill and mocking.

'Why did you come? I would have thought our honeymoon was enough to put you off the place for life!'

His blue eyes met hers as coldly as twin laser beams. Shrugging slightly, he picked up a bottle of Indonesian beer and prised off the lid with an opener. Then he took a couple of leisurely gulps before replying.

'True,' he said indifferently. 'But Bali is a beautiful place. It would have been plain stupid to let one set of bad memories spoil it for me forever. After all, our honeymoon wasn't all that important, was it? Not when you weigh it against the rest of our lives.'

'No,' she retorted with a nonchalance that was totally counterfeit. 'No, I suppose it wasn't all that important. Look, how about passing me a drink too?'

She drank a bottle of fizzy lemon squash and ate two chicken sandwiches and a banana in a valiant attempt not to seem upset. Yet inside her an aching misery was settling like lead in the pit of her stomach. Not important? Until now she had always believed that marrying Richard was the most important thing she had done in her life. Even after all the anger and pain he had brought her, it made her feel hurt and belittled to have their honeymoon brushed aside as meaningless. Not important, she thought bitterly. Right. Thank you, Richard, for reminding me of how insensitive you are. It'll make it easier for me to close my heart to you.

'There's not much point in stopping for lunch at Penelokan, is there?' she demanded coolly. 'I seem to remember that it was a bit dull apart from the view. Anyway those sandwiches have taken the edge off my appetite.'

'Just as you like,' shrugged Richard. 'But let's push on anyway.'

The road wound up through Bangli and the thick vegetation shut off the view so that they saw nothing of the country they were approaching until they suddenly drove through a ceremonial gateway and found it laid out beneath them like a contoured map. What they were seeing was a large caldera ten or eleven kilometres across, filled with an improbably vivid blue lake and rimmed by rugged hills carpeted with lush green vegetation. Penelokan and, below it, Lake Batur.

'Well, even if you don't want lunch, at the very least I need a cup of coffee,' announced Richard, turning off the road into the car park of a café. 'Are you going to join me or not?'

As they walked across from the car to the building, he draped his arm casually round her shoulders and she stiffened, hoping that he could not feel the violent beating of her heart. It was over there, there on that very outcrop of hillside with the trees plummeting down to the blue lake below, that he had kissed her! Back when life was simple and she believed in happy endings. Biting her lip, she allowed him to steer her to a table on the deck with a panoramic view of the haunting landscape below.

'Two coffees, please—one black with two sugars, one white, without.'

He gazed calmly out over the blue expanse of water beneath them and smiled at her.

'Nice view, isn't it?' he commented pleasantly.

Emma stared at him in stupefaction as the truth slowly dawned on her. He hadn't brought her through some extreme refinement of cruelty at all. No! Richard wasn't planning to watch with amusement as she agonised over old memories. Nothing so subtle. He had simply forgotten the entire incident. Forgotten...how he had kissed her...what he had said to her...how they had felt...

The swine! The heartless, callous, unfeeling, disloyal swine!

'Yes, it's lovely,' she said drily. 'Do you think I could have my coffee extra strong?'

After twenty minutes they continued on their way down the road which zigzagged until it reached the lake's edge, then hugged the shoreline, bumping along until they reached Air Panas. Here Richard parked the car outside the same hotel they had stayed in nine years before, but by now Emma was awake to his tactics and had her reactions firmly under control. No way would she let the faintest flicker of nostalgia or regret appear in her face. Instead she wore only a look of mild interest as they went into the hotel and signed the register. A smiling teenage girl led them to a simple room with rattan walls and nothing but the most basic furniture. Emma's faint aura of boredom slipped slightly when she realised there was only one bed but she knew it was useless to make a fuss. At least the room was clean and had a proper *en-suite* bathroom. And if Richard was really intent on ravishing her like some medieval villain, presumably he could have done it just as well in the luxury hotel back at Sanur.

Fortunately Richard's mind seemed to be on other things than medieval ravishment. Tossing the two overnight bags on the floor, he walked over to the window and looked out at the view which it framed—an attractive, gentle vista of flowering trees, green grass and the blue waters of the lake.

'How about a walk round the foreshore?' he suggested. 'And then we could have a swim in the hot-springs pool before dinner.'

'All right,' agreed Emma.

It was very pleasant walking along the shore of the lake and her pretence of composure gave way to genuine enjoyment. Because of the hot springs the water in this

area was quite warm and Emma took off her sandals
and paddled for a while, frisking like a child, kicking
up arcs of water just for the pleasure of watching the
rainbow droplets sparkle in the sun. Richard didn't join
her, but stood smiling indulgently and shaking his head.
When she emerged, she felt almost as if she had come
here simply for fun. They must have walked ten or twelve
kilometres, most of the time in companionable silence,
but occasionally breaking into speech to discuss what
they saw around them. A small group of Balinese cows,
as pretty and graceful as deer with their caramel-coloured
coats and liquid brown eyes, standing in the shallows
being washed by a small boy. A toothless old lady with
a face as brown and wrinkled as a walnut carrying a
pyramid of offerings on her head to lay in front of a
wayside shrine. A couple of fishermen out on the water
in shallow canoes who waved a greeting at them. By the
time they headed back for the hotel, Emma felt
comfortably relaxed and weary.

'And now for our evening bath,' announced Richard,
with a hint of laughter in his voice.

She understood the laughter when they arrived at the
hot springs to find fifty or sixty of the local villagers
already companionably stretched out in the water, gos-
siping and laughing. Some of them had brought along
packets of soap powder and dirty clothes and were
pounding their washing in the shallows while they chat-
tered to their friends. In the west, the flaming red ball
of the sun was preparing to sink behind the mountain.
Emma stared in disbelief at the scene before her and
started to giggle.

'I just don't believe it,' she said. 'It's so strange, so
unexpected, somehow. Like having a party in your
laundry.'

'I know,' agreed Richard with a chuckle. 'It's one of
the things I love about Bali, the way the people do

everything with such gusto. Life, death, art, work, play, they throw themselves into everything with this amazing energy and humour and goodwill. And although they don't have a quarter of our possessions they seem to have the happiness that eludes so many of us.'

His face was sombre for an instant, then he gripped her hand and led her down to the pool.

'Come on,' he urged. 'The water's fine.'

It was fine. In fact it was an amazingly peaceful and relaxing experience to lie there in the warm water, surrounded by the musical rise and fall of voices, watching the sky change from a blazing crimson to a deep purple velvet and occasionally casting a shy, darting glance at Richard by her side. However much she might try to tell herself that she hated him, she could not suppress a thrill of pride at the powerful, tanned, masculine body that lurked beside her in the water. To her surprise, Richard seemed to understand quite a lot of the language and he chatted fluently to the villagers, his white teeth gleaming in the gathering darkness and his deep baritone laugh ringing out over the silent water. At last Emma rose to her feet and gazed regretfully down at herself.

'I have to get out,' she announced. 'I'm turning into a prune.'

Richard too surged out of the water, a bronzed god from the deep, and took her hand.

'An albino prune,' he commented, lifting her hand to his eyes in the uncertain light. 'You're awfully pale, Emma. Haven't you been out in the sun at all this summer?'

'No, I've been too busy. What with this threatened collapse of Prero's and everything, I've hardly even been outside of my office.'

His hand tightened on hers but he said nothing until half an hour later when they had showered and changed and were sitting outside waiting for their dinner. Brightly coloured lamps were strung along the edges of the deck and a moon the size and colour of a pumpkin had risen over the lake. Somewhere in the background a gamelan orchestra could be heard tuning up for the night's session of traditional dancing, which Richard and Emma had decided not to attend. The air was cool and still and filled with the scent of flowers. Richard had ordered a bottle of champagne and, to Emma's surprise, he raised the first glass in a solemn toast to her.

'Well, here's to you, Emma,' he said. 'And to Prero's.'

'To Prero's,' agreed Emma in a subdued voice.

But the foolish thought rose in her mind that she would much rather have been drinking a toast to the pair of them. She sipped slowly at the prickly, bubbling liquid and eyed him thoughtfully.

'You don't seem too enthused about it,' commented Richard drily. 'Is it the champagne itself or Prero's that you're not keen on?'

'The champagne's fine,' she said hastily. 'And I'm very grateful that Prero's is going to continue trading too. I would have hated to think of all those people being put out of work. But sometimes, Richard, I wish I'd never inherited the damned business. You can't imagine what a burden it's been.'

'Oh, yes, I can,' retorted Richard grimly. 'I've been in business for myself nearly twenty years now, remember, and I know it isn't a piece of cake. But I've got to hand it to you, Emma, you did a damn fine job with Prero's. It can't have been easy for you, taking over when you were only twenty-one.'

'No, it wasn't,' agreed Emma, grateful for his understanding. 'I'd had an expensive and largely useless education and I knew more about flower-arranging than I did about balance sheets, so suddenly being thrown into being a major property developer was the most terrifying thing that had ever happened in my life. And some

of those construction crews weren't too keen on having
a woman as boss, I can tell you. It was pretty alarming
to deal with all those rough, macho men.'

Richard gave a sudden growl of laughter.

'Well, you didn't seem to have any trouble dealing
with rough, macho men when you met me,' he pointed
out. 'Heavens, I can remember you coming out on the
back terrace at your father's house carrying a tray of
cold beer cans as if you'd been a barmaid for the last
twenty years. I remember thinking to myself, That's a
girl in a million. Not only does she look terrific, but she
reads minds. You didn't seem at all alarmed then.'

Emma gave a splutter of laughter at the memory.

'That's all you know!' she replied. 'I really had to
work up my courage to go out and confront you all. But
I felt so sorry for you, working in that heat. Besides,
you and your crew were different from a lot of the men
I've met since. You were really polite to me.'

Her thoughts strayed back and she remembered
Richard, a tall, blond giant, naked to the waist, tanned
and sweaty and incredibly handsome, directing a crew
of workers who were building an extension on to her
father's house. Taking pity on them in the fierce heat,
Emma had carried drinks to them and later Richard had
returned to the kitchen door with the empty tray. Her
heart had done back-flips at the sight of him and she
hadn't known where to look in her embarrassment. As
if he was sharing the memory, Richard smiled too, an
odd, brooding smile.

'Well, my politeness didn't do you much good with
your father, did it?' he demanded. 'I seem to remember
that when he found out you'd been soiling your fair
hands giving drinks to the labourers he went right off
his head.'

'No, he wasn't too pleased,' she admitted, even though
it made her flinch to remember how her father had

stormed around the house, slamming his fist on furniture, shouting at her about her position and prospects and badmouthing the workmen outside. All because she had offered them drinks on a hot day. 'Did you hear all that?'

'Yes, I did,' said Richard grimly. 'And it was a toss-up whether I'd finish laying the ridge-pole, or go inside and punch him in the jaw for speaking to you like that. My God, he was an old devil! But he didn't manage to stop you sneaking out to the rock concert with me the following week, did he?'

Emma smiled guiltily.

'No,' she said, shaking her head. 'I remember now. You heard me playing that Nec Plus Ultra tape and asked me if I knew that they were doing a live concert the following week at the big cricket ground. I couldn't believe it when you invited me to go with you.'

Richard leaned back in his chair and a reminiscent smile spread over his face.

'Yes, I guess that was the start of it,' he mused. 'Or maybe it was the picnic at Manly the week after. That's right! I kissed you under the Norfolk pines on the esplanade. There's no need to blush like that, Emma. My intentions were honourable and I kept myself under very strict control whenever I was with you, remember?'

Emma flushed. Yes, it was true. In fact, she had actually been a virgin when she married, although certainly not through her own choice. It was Richard who had put the brakes on as their relationship had grown more heated. Richard who, with an unexpected streak of puritanism, had insisted on marriage before consummating their relationship. Although, heaven knew, they had more than made up for lost time after the wedding... Blushing even more deeply, Emma gave him a quick, shy glance.

'Why did you insist on waiting?' she demanded. 'You know I would have gone to bed with you if you'd given me the slightest encouragement.'

Richard's eyebrows drew together in a stormy frown and he gazed at her with piercing blue eyes.

'I know that,' he growled. 'And don't think I wasn't tempted. But I didn't want to take advantage of you, Emma. You were so young, so totally inexperienced.'

Emma tossed her head rebelliously, sending her long hair swinging over her shoulders.

'Not totally!' she protested. 'There was a Swiss ski instructor who kissed me at an *après-ski* party behind the chalet when I was seventeen.'

'I'd rather not hear about that,' said Richard in a dangerous voice. 'Although I can well imagine that you were a handful even before I met you. But however passionate your nature, you were still so innocent, so incredibly vulnerable. And I didn't want to be the one to hurt you. God knows, I felt guilty enough marrying you when you were so young. I couldn't have lived with myself if I'd urged you into a sexual relationship without marriage. I wanted you to know that I was committed, that I really cared, took you seriously.'

It was absurd, sentimental, ridiculous. The kind of thing that men must have said to women back before the First World War. And yet his words made her feel like marshmallow inside. Smiling mistily, she reached out and laid her fingers over his.

'Thank you,' she said softly.

Richard drew his hand away from hers as if he had been stung and his fingers drummed threateningly on the edge of the table.

'Well, it just shows you what a fool I was, doesn't it?' he rasped. 'Putting you on a pedestal was the worst mistake I've ever made in my life. But it's not one I'll repeat. I should have had enough sense to realise that all you wanted from me was sex and a way of escaping from under your father's thumb. Well, I've learnt my lesson. This time I'll handle things the way I should have done in the first place. I'll have a short, passionate affair with you and then it will be goodbye.'

Emma stared at him aghast, feeling as hurt as if he had leaned forward and slapped her face. Heaven knew she didn't want him to put her on a pedestal! But she didn't want him treating her with this cold, scornful disdain either. And, as for his scathing assessment of her motives for marrying him, it made her so furious that she longed to reach forward and slap *him* in the face. Instead she replied in a cool, brittle voice, 'Suits me, darling. Except that I could do without the affair. Personally, I never go back to a discarded lover. Once the magic is over, what's the point?'

Richard gritted his teeth with an audible grinding sound and his blue eyes smouldered at her. For a moment she thought she had gone too far and felt a delicious, quaking feeling of terror as to what he might do, but fortunately the waitress chose that moment to arrive with the dinner.

The food was good. Savoury chicken in creamy coconut sauce with noodles and steamed vegetables, followed by crisp banana fritters. Yet there was little scintillating dinner-party conversation to go with it. Richard ate in murderous silence, handling his knife and fork as if they were dangerous weapons. When they had finished the meal, instead of escorting her back to their room, he rose to his feet and announced abruptly that he was going for a walk. Without a backward glance he strode off towards the lakeside, his long, athletic stride eating up the ground.

Emma told herself she didn't care. Making her way back to their room, she undressed, lay down on the bed and defiantly picked up a fat paperback book which she proceeded to read as if her life depended on it. For the first twenty minutes she was so preoccupied that she could not have said whether it was a spy thriller or a treatise on botany, but little by little her interest was caught. After a while she forgot all about Richard and became absorbed in the story so that it was a surprise to her when she finally looked at her small travelling clock and saw that it was well after one o'clock in the morning. For a moment she felt a pang of alarm, worrying whether something had happened to him, but then reason asserted itself. Probably he was just out there walking off his bad temper. Well, she certainly wasn't going to pursue him and try to make things right between them! At least she had enough sense to know that that was a lost cause.

Tossing the book on to the floor, she flicked off the light and closed her eyes. The deep, velvety night descended on her like the wings of some huge, dark bird and she drifted into sleep... Hours later, she woke in the soft glow of the bedside lamp to find Richard shaking her. Groggy and protesting, she fought her way up to the surface of wakefulness.

'What's wrong? What do you want? What's happened?'

'It's time you got up. I want to reach the rim of the crater before the weather gets too hot.'

Blinking and shuddering, Emma hauled herself upright and looked at her clock.

'But it's only five-thirty!' she protested.

'The best time to start,' insisted Richard firmly, stripping the bedcover off her with a ruthless gesture. 'Now, can you take a shower alone, or do you need help?'

That threat was enough to get her moving and half an hour later, after a breakfast of rice cakes and fruit, they were on their way up the lane that led from the centre of the village towards the mountain. Once they passed the little temple about a kilometre from the village the sun rose abruptly among the hills, flooding the scene with brilliant red-gold light. They continued across the cindery scrubland at the base of the mountain, traversed a couple of dry riverbeds and headed for the peak. Now the way became very steep and dusty and in several places Emma had to grasp at the small pine trees that grew beside the track to get a hand-hold. Their sharp fragrance clung to her skin and her breath began to come in deep, laboured gulps. Although the air was cool and fresh, her mint-green polo shirt was turning dark with sweat and clinging to her body, while her legs were dusty and her shorts streaked with mud. All the same, she could not suppress an unexpected feeling of exhilaration as she toiled up the slope behind Richard. If only there had not been so much tension between them, she would have been enjoying every minute of this.

When at last the path divided, they took the left-hand branch down to the lower point of the crater rim and were met by the welcome sight of two boys selling cold soft drinks. Fortified with fizzy lemon, they set off again for the high point of the crater rim. Here the track was narrow and precipitous, with steep drops on either side and dizzying views over waterfalls and gorges covered with lush green foliage. More than once Richard had to take her hand and coax her along, as she darted nervous glances at the ground plummeting away below, but he did this with an impersonal kindness that chilled her. There was none of the eye contact, none of the warm, special smiles that there had been on their honeymoon, and when at last they reached the crater rim Richard did not put his arm around her. Instead he stood apart from her with his arms folded, gazing down with a brooding expression at the scene below.

The first time she had come here Emma had been thrilled by the magnificence of the sight. Now she felt oppressed by the eerie silence, broken only by the occasional ominous sound of a rock crashing into the crater or the forlorn cry of a bird. Wreaths of steam rose soundlessly from clefts in the rock and the air had a faint sulphurous tang to it. Last time she was here Richard had kissed her again and again, had crushed her in his arms and told her how much it meant to him to share this strange, exotic place with her. Now they seemed to be sharing nothing except an intense mutual dislike. Richard stood apart from her, eyeing her askance with an odd, bitter smile hovering on his lips. There seemed no point at all to the expedition.

'Can't we go now?' she burst out fretfully.

He shrugged.

'Yes. Well. I suppose we've achieved the aim of the expedition,' he replied drily. 'Let's get back.'

They took a different path coming back, one which was even steeper than the first, and Emma had little attention to spare for anything other than simple survival, particularly since Richard now seemed to be ignoring her entirely. He hurried on ahead with demonic energy, only turning back occasionally to make sure that she was still in sight before hurtling down another steep stretch of terrain. By the time they reached the hotel again, Emma was exhausted, filthy and in a thoroughly bad temper.

'I'm going to take a shower,' she announced flatly and disappeared into the bathroom, slamming and locking the door.

Deliberately she took her time, washing her hair and even waxing her legs and manicuring her nails, taking a malicious pleasure in keeping Richard waiting. But when she emerged in a cool cotton frock, she found that he was no longer wearing his sweat-stained shorts and

T-shirt. In fact, she realised with mounting alarm, he was wearing nothing at all. He stood balanced on his right leg, with his left leg braced against the bed as he vigorously towelled it dry. As if drawn by magnetism, Emma's gaze travelled up that hard brown muscular thigh with its flecks of bronze hair to the fork of his body. Instinctively she caught her breath. Richard glanced up sharply at the sound.

'Wh-what are you doing?' she faltered.

'What does it look as if I'm doing?' he snapped. 'You looked as though you were planning to stay in the bathroom half the night so I went for a swim in the thermal springs. I'm just getting dried.'

'Oh.'

In spite of her best intentions, she stole another swift, furtive glance at him and then blushed hotly at the unmistakable signs of his growing arousal. Hastily she averted her eyes and her stricken gaze met his.

'Of course, there are other things I could do,' he said throatily, flinging away the towel.

Emma's whole body stiffened and her heart gave a tumultuous leap of terror and excitement.

'What do you mean?' she demanded, backing away.

He crossed the room slowly, tauntingly.

'You know damned well what I mean,' he growled. Then, winding her long, dark hair around his fingers, he reeled her in like a fish on the end of a line. 'Why don't we find out if the magic really is over, Emma?'

CHAPTER FIVE

EMMA opened her mouth to protest and found it stopped by a long, hungry kiss. Richard's naked body was pressed hard against her and she could feel the power in his tense, bunched muscles as he hauled her more fiercely into his embrace. His legs were straddled wide apart, engulfing her in a way that made her feel small, fragile, infinitely feminine. Through the thin cotton of her dress she could feel the heat radiating from his body in waves and with it came a faint, salty, masculine odour that made her head swim. An answering warmth leapt through her own veins and she gave a small, shuddering sigh as his mouth left hers and moved down her throat in a trail of scorching kisses. With frenzied urgency he unbuttoned the front of her dress, revealing her soft white breasts budded with pink. Slipping his hands inside her bodice, he stroked them teasingly until they rose in hard, aroused peaks. Then, with a swift, abrupt movement, he withdrew his fingers and snatched at the sides of her dress, crumpling the fabric into balls.

'Take it off,' he ordered hoarsely.

'No!'

'Yes!'

There was a sharp sound of ripping cloth, a muffled loss of breath as the dress was hauled savagely over her head and flung away. Then Emma found herself naked and shrinking under Richard's intent, glittering gaze. Instinctively she flung up her hands to cover her breasts and opened her mouth to voice a protest. But Richard's fingers covered her lips, then moved over her cheeks in an unexpectedly tender caress.

'Don't fight me, sweetheart,' he growled. 'It's been so long. Far, far too long. Let me look at you... touch you... in the old, special ways...'

As he spoke, his hands were rippling down over her hair and shoulders, prising her defensive fingers loose and raising them to be kissed. With a slow, provocative smile he drew one of her fingers into his mouth and sucked softly on it so that a tremulous thrill of warmth shot through her entire body. She shuddered and her eyes closed briefly. She had always loved it when he did that. Loved it too when his fingers crept down her spine in those firm, caressing circles as they were doing now... Loved it when he kissed her... oh, so softly... on her ear so that his warm breath sent tingles of excitement flaring through her. Yes. Yes. Like that. An involuntary pang of pure sensual ecstasy shafted through her and she uttered a soft moan.

'Well, do you want me to stop?' he murmured, his mouth so close that his breath stirred her hair.

Her body was arched into his, her head was tilted back and her breasts were strained against his chest, brushing against his warm, hard muscles in a way that she found unbearably arousing. Every cell in her body seemed to be tingling and a long-forgotten heat was pulsing through her in dizzying waves. Oh, heavens, how she wanted him! Her whole body seemed to be a throbbing ache of need, which only intensified when Richard pulled her ruthlessly against him. She could feel the stirring of his male warmth, the damp, hot urgency of his passion as he ground her body against his.

'Well, do you want me to stop?' he repeated in a low, taunting growl.

She heard the mockery in his voice and did not care. Did not care about anything except the one primitive fact that this was her man, her husband, naked and hard and virile, crushing her in his arms and demanding her total submission. And she needed him, wanted him, loved him with a blind and reckless violence that destroyed all sense of self-preservation.

'Answer me!' he challenged again.

'No,' she choked, collapsing against him in a shuddering surrender. 'Damn you! You know I don't want you to stop...'

A gleam of triumph narrowed his blue eyes and twisted the corners of his mouth. Suddenly, with a swift movement, he scooped her into his arms and stood gazing down at her, exulting in his victory.

'Good,' he murmured hoarsely. 'Then I'm going to carry you over to that bed, Emma, and enjoy you until you beg for mercy.'

She stiffened resentfully at the gloating tone in his voice. Why did he take such pleasure in forcing her to admit how much she wanted him? Obviously he enjoyed humiliating her by dragging the admission out of her. And that must mean that he did not, could not possibly love her any longer, for otherwise he would never want to hurt her like this. For an instant she hated him so much that she wanted to slap the mocking smile off his face. Yet, as he dumped her carelessly on the bed and crouched above her with a look of brooding triumph, she discovered that rage could be a powerful aphrodisiac. She hated him, hated him! And yet, glancing nervously at his powerful, masculine figure looming over her, she wanted him with an urgency that appalled her. The bedside lamp glowed like orange firelight on his skin, highlighting every muscle and sinew and making his body hair glow like copper wire. In its haunting glow, with his gleaming eyes and wildly disordered blond curls, he looked like some primitive caveman. And the responses which he awoke in Emma were equally primitive.

'Time enough for preliminaries in the future,' he murmured brutally. 'Tonight, I'm simply going to take you, ready or not.' His hand rubbed down over her breasts and belly in a casual gesture of ownership and then explored further. 'But it seems as if you are ready, doesn't it, Emma? More than ready. Begging for it.'

Anger scorched through her, but he spoke the simple truth. And when he lowered his crushing, masculine weight on to her and drove into her with ruthless force, her treacherous body welcomed him gladly. Turning away her face and twisting in agitation, she tried to remember that she hated him, but all she cold feel was a wild, breathless rejoicing at his return. They belonged together, like this, with their bodies moving in a frantic, intoxicating rhythm of passion and love and mutual need. Oh, yes, yes, yes, yes, my love, my darling! she sang inside her head. Oh, God, I've been so miserable without you. Don't leave me, please, please don't ever leave me! Yet by digging her nails into her palms and clamping her lips tightly closed she somehow held back the reckless, dangerous words. Until the very end. For when those dazzling, electrical pulses of sensation suddenly burst into flames and made her whole body convulse in ecstasy, all restraint vanished. Shocked and exalted, she found that she was clinging to Richard, whimpering and gasping and babbling what she had most wanted to hide.

'Richard. Oh, my darling! I love you. I love you!'

His response took her by surprise. Threading his strong fingers through her hair, he crushed her against him, holding her as if he would never let her go. She felt the wild thudding of his heart, heard his low moan of fulfilment as he too reached his climax and then collapsed, spent and shuddering, on top of her.

'Emma…Emma,' he breathed hoarsely. 'Oh, Emma.'

She smiled secretively into his warm, damp shoulder, then reached out and snapped off the light. As they lay exhausted and intertwined, a deep, solemn happiness welled up inside her. He hadn't told her in so many words that he still loved her, but hope blazed inside her. Magically their lovemaking seemed to have changed everything and the way Richard had held her, the way he had gasped her name made her feel that everything was bound to come right between them. In the velvety blackness she heard his breath slow and quieten. With a joyful smile, she wriggled out from beneath him and turned on her side so that she could nestle into the crook of his arm. For a long time she lay awake, too exhilarated and wound up to sleep, but at last she drifted into darkness. Her last thought was filled with dreamy pleasure. We will stay together, I know we will...

But Emma's optimism was short-lived. She woke the following morning with the uncomfortable sensation that she was being watched. Sleepily opening her eyes, she saw that Richard was already dressed and sitting in a cane chair next to the bed, gazing down at her with a strange, brooding expression on his face. His chin rested on his hand and something about the tense stillness of his pose made her suspect that he had been there for hours. An ominous thrill of alarm ran through her limbs and she stretched out her hand to him, groping for reassurance.

'Darling, what's wrong?' she began. 'Have you——?'

'Don't waste your cheap endearments on me!' he retorted savagely. Then, surging to his feet, he prowled across the room and snarled at her over his shoulder, 'Get dressed. We're taking the first plane we can get back to Australia.'

Thoroughly alarmed now, Emma scrambled out of bed and ran after him. Laying one hand imploringly on his arm, she dragged him round to face her.

'Richard! What's wrong? Everything was going so well last night! I thought you loved me again!'

His blue eyes scanned her naked body with a gaze so contemptuous that it scorched her. Scornfully, deliberately he looked up from her heaving breasts to her face.

'Then you thought wrongly,' he hissed. 'And I'd rather you didn't mention the word "love" between us again, Emma. After all, it's pretty debased currency where you're concerned, isn't it? I'm sure you've gasped out the same touching little confession to at least half a dozen other men. I suppose you think it adds an extra edge to the sexual frenzy, do you?'

'No!' cried Emma in horror. 'No! Richard, how can you say such dreadful things?'

His voice was like velvet now—husky, gently abrasive, with a softness that was indefinably menacing.

'Easily, Emma,' he purred. 'Just as easily as you can mouth your smooth, lying professions of love to me. But I prefer the clean, cold truth. What we shared last night wasn't love, it was just a damned good——'

She winced at the crudity of the word as if he had seared her flesh with a whiplash. Then, with wide, horrified eyes, she backed away from him, shaking her head in a dazed fashion as she fought to understand what he meant.

'No!' she protested hoarsely, her throat so tight that she could hardly utter the words. 'No, Richard. It may have been for you, but it wasn't for me.'

'You lying little whore!'

Her chin came up and her face flamed.

'If that's what you think of me, then release me from this ridiculous agreement!' she challenged. 'You've had what you wanted, you've proved your point. Now let me go!'

Dimly she recognised that Richard was in an even worse state of torment than she was herself. Every muscle and contour of his powerful, masculine physique radiated tension and aggression. His legs were planted wide apart, his fists were clenched, a threatening scowl disfigured his face and his breath came in shallow, rapid gulps as if he had been running a long-distance race. Yet even now he clung stubbornly to his outrageous purpose.

'No!' he growled through clenched teeth. 'I said three months and three months it will be.'

Emma felt the end of the bed touch the back of her leg and suddenly could bear no more. She sat down with a groan and saw that Richard's gaze was still fixed on her naked body with a hungry, disturbing ferocity. Fumbling on the floor, she found a crumpled dressing-gown and shrugged herself into it. Then she straightened up and looked him dead in the eye. It was like clashing swords with an antagonist whose only aim was to strike at the heart. For the first time she realised just how much pent-up rage and hostility Richard felt towards her and she was baffled and dismayed by the force of it. Why? Why did he hate her so much? Her first impulse was to fling on her clothes and flee back to Sydney where she could be alone with her turbulent feelings. But what would that achieve? In any case, she was no longer a shy nineteen-year-old, but a hardened businesswoman, the veteran of countless boardroom battles. Tossing back her long, dark hair, she squared her shoulders and spoke.

'All right, Richard,' she said evenly. 'You've made it clear what you want. Now it's my turn to state my demands. I am not a whore. I'm your wife. But if you can't accord me the respect and love that should go with that position, at the very least there is something else that I demand from you.'

'What's that?' growled Richard suspiciously.

Emma flashed him a bitter smile.

'Common courtesy,' she replied. 'Whether we're alone or in public, from now on you treat me with as much courtesy as if I'm an honoured guest. Otherwise I'll walk out, bargain or no bargain. Do I make myself clear?'

'Perfectly clear,' sneered Richard. 'You've come on a lot, Emma, since the days when you were a bashful teenager. I must say I find it hard not to admire you.'

'Try,' invited Emma coolly. 'I don't want your admiration, Richard. Just simple good manners. Now, do we have a deal or not?'

He gave her a long, hard look that was compounded of resentment and a reluctantly dawning amusement. Then unexpectedly he offered her a formal handshake.

'I suppose we do,' he agreed.

Yet it wasn't a complete victory for Emma, since Richard's notion of courtesy and hers seemed to be poles apart. On the drive to the airport he remained silent and uncommunicative and even on the flight back to Australia there was no improvement in his temper. Whenever Emma spoke to him, he either ignored her or snapped her head off. At last, feeling hurt and infuriated, she was driven to raise the difficult topic of what they were to do when they reached Sydney.

'Look, I think it would be best if I just took a taxi from the airport to my place when we arrive. I know you said we should stay together but I——'

She got no further.

'Don't be ridiculous,' retorted Richard. 'You'll come to my house as we agreed, so there's no more to be said. In any case, I've already arranged for Amanda to move your belongings there and meet us with a car when we arrive.'

An inexplicable feeling of apprehension gripped her.

'Who's Amanda?' she asked.

Emma found out the answer to that question when they arrived at Sydney Airport. A tall, blonde woman of about thirty in an expensive and deceptively simple cream linen dress came gliding across to meet them with a welcoming smile pinned to her lips. Close up, Emma saw that her hair was cut rather short and spiky in a fashionably aggressive style and that her blue eyes were shrewd and assessing.

'Hello, Richard,' she said in a husky contralto. 'Did you have a good trip?'

'Very nice,' confirmed Richard non-committally. 'Amanda, I don't believe you've met my wife Emma. Emma, this is Amanda Morris—a lawyer with my firm.'

Emma thought she saw Amanda flinch briefly at the mention of the word 'wife', but her smile was pleasant, although it did not touch her blue eyes.

'How do you do, Emma?'

'Hello,' said Emma uncomfortably.

Amanda looked fresh and crisp and elegant, the well-cut dress showing off her deep suntan and her face carefully made up. In contrast Emma suddenly felt more crumpled and sweaty and travel-stained than ever. She was not feeling well either, although it was probably just jet-lag—long flights always did upset her—so she didn't protest when Amanda simply took over the organisation of everything. And she had to admit that Amanda was efficient. Within five minutes of leaving the main terminus building they were ensconced in a large white limousine with their baggage stowed in the boot.

'You might be more comfortable in the back, Emma,' said Amanda, opening the door for her. 'You'll have more room in there. And I'm afraid I'm going to have to talk shop with Richard on the way.'

What she was saying was reasonable enough, but Emma could not help feeling a spurt of annoyance as she was bundled into the back like a piece of extra luggage, while Richard climbed into the front next to Amanda. The young woman drove fast and skilfully, but she seemed to have the capacity to do two things equally well at the same time. As the streets of Sydney flashed past them, the talk flew backwards and forwards between Richard and Amanda of a new shopping centre in the outer suburbs, a hitch in the exchange of contracts and a possible need for expensive litigation. Emma leaned back in her seat and shuddered. She was perfectly well-qualified to join in the discussion herself, having attended countless board meetings on similar topics, but she simply couldn't be bothered. At this moment business was the last thing on her mind. What was making her stomach churn nervously was pure and simple worry about her relationship with Richard.

Deep down she still felt stubbornly convinced that the old, familiar fires of love raged in both of them. That last night in Bali she had been certain that Richard loved her as passionately as ever. Not that he had told her so in words, but how often had Richard ever done that? His spoken admissions of love had never been anything but rare and grudging, as if torn out of him by forces beyond his control. Yet there were other ways of communicating than by mere words. And the way Richard had hauled her so violently against him, the fierce, intent light in his eyes when he'd gazed at her, the urgent pressure of his lips and hands had all told her in their own secret way that he still loved her. Which had made it all the more of a shock to be woken the next day to meet with hostility and sarcasm.

Emma grimaced, recalling the scene. Could she possibly have been wrong? What if Richard didn't love her any more and his own explanation was the simple truth? Could he really be so vindictive as to seduce her purely for revenge? And did he seriously expect her to go and live with him for the next three months? Would he stick to his agreement to treat her politely or would he go back to hurling cruel, unfounded insults at her? And what was his relationship with Amanda? Was she only his employee? Or did she mean more to him than that?

It was a relief when at last the car turned into a driveway of a Mediterranean-style villa set in an acre of gardens overlooking the harbour. Through a tangled wilderness of overgrown trees, bushes and flowering plants Emma caught tantalising glimpses of a large house with pumpkin-coloured stucco walls, green shutters and an orange pantile roof. The gravel driveway was overgrown in places with weeds, but to Emma's experienced eye it was immediately clear that the garden had once been beautiful and cherished. Palm trees stood like architectural columns amid a lawn of buffalo grass whose centrepiece was a stone fountain with a statuette of a boy and a dolphin in the centre, although weeds choked the dry pool beneath. Pale blue plumbago flowers rioted in a sort of hedge along one boundary of the lawn, while the air was sweet with the fragrance of numerous frangipani bushes. Fortunately, at least while Amanda was with them, Richard seemed to be mindful of his promise about courtesy.

'It's gone to seed a bit,' he remarked, twisting in his seat to look at Emma. 'So I thought you might like to advise me on restoring it and also find a suitable place for those Balinese garden statues we bought. There's a conservatory too at the back of the house overlooking the harbour. Half the glass panes are smashed but they could be fixed up. Maybe you can organise some tradesmen to tackle it.'

Emma was silent for a moment, chewing her lip. It made her feel deeply uncomfortable to have Richard trying to draw her into his plans for restoring the house and garden, especially when she knew they were only going to have three months together. Was it just some malicious game he was playing with her? Or did he really want to involve her in his life? She longed to demand the truth from him but felt constrained by Amanda's presence in the car. Instead she fell back on safe, neutral ground.

'How long have you owned the house?' she asked.

'Only three months. It was a deceased's estate. An old lady lived here and she was too feeble to keep the place up near the end. But I think once it's restored it will be a fine home.'

Emma couldn't help agreeing with this assessment when Richard led her inside the house. The interior had the same air of rather shabby grandeur as the garden. A huge chandelier lit the vast, mosaic-tiled entrance hall and a marble staircase with black wrought-iron banisters led to the storey upstairs. But the cream, embossed wallpaper had large patches of damp and was torn in places while the air held the stale, musty scent of long disuse. Richard dumped their suitcases unceremoniously on the floor in front of an ornate, carved Italian credenza topped by a flamboyant, gilt-edged mirror. Then he turned to Amanda.

'Thanks for meeting us at the airport,' he said pleasantly. 'I guess it's time you got back to the office now, though.'

'I can stay if there's anything else you need done,' offered Amanda.

'No, that's all right,' replied Richard, smiling in a way that made his eyes crinkle at the edges. 'You've done far too much for us already.'

Emma felt a pang of jealousy as fierce as the stabbing of a knife at the look Amanda gave him at these words. She's in love with him, she thought. It's written all over her. But what does he feel for her? As the door closed behind the other woman, Emma tried to hide her misgivings. If Richard really was in love with Amanda, Emma knew she would be a fool to give free rein to her own feelings for him. Their reunion in Bali had shown her vividly that their sexual passion still blazed as fiercely as ever, but she was no longer a nineteen-year-old bride. These days she wasn't fool enough to think that love and sex were the only keys needed for a happy marriage. All the love and sex in the world wouldn't save her from heartbreak if she still couldn't trust Richard. And was it really likely that she could? She thought again of the look that had passed between Richard and Amanda and a mounting sense of uneasiness rose inside her.

'How will she get back to the office?' she asked abruptly.

'Well, she left her own car here,' replied Richard. 'She often does. Now, do you want to look around the house?'

'Not right now,' protested Emma. 'What I'd really like at the moment is a shower and a cup of tea.'

Richard nodded. His earlier surliness in Bali and on the flight home had vanished. Yet in its place there was now an elaborate courtesy in his manner which she found equally off-putting. It was as if he had finally subjugated his hatred for her and could now view her quite calmly as if she were nothing but a temporary guest. But the thought didn't bring her much comfort. Damn it! She didn't want to be treated as if she were a business acquaintance. She was his wife, not a visitor! And if it took one of their rip-roaring, tumultuous quarrels—complete with upraised voices, slammed doors and swinging picture frames—to break down the barriers between them, then so be it. For an instant she yearned with all her heart for the old, familiar Richard, raging from room to room like an angry bear. Then her eyes met his and the hope died. An awful, twisting misery gripped Emma's stomach as she realised she was staring at a total stranger. Someone who happened to share her husband's tousled, blond curls, vivid blue eyes and towering physique, but who looked at her with an indifference that was wholly alien.

'Come upstairs and I'll show you the bedroom,' he invited. 'At least that's been renovated. That and the kitchen were the first things I tackled.'

Emma followed him up the stairs to a vast bedroom overlooking the harbour which was shrouded in near-total darkness. Crossing the room, he opened internal wooden shutters then glass French doors and finally long, external wooden shutters which he hitched back on a balcony outside. A flood of sunshine and fresh air swept into the room and Emma saw that it had indeed been renovated. The walls were covered with a white, embossed wallpaper, while the thick green carpet underfoot was as soft and luxurious as a bed of moss. Yet it was the bed which dominated the whole room. It was a huge mahogany edifice surmounted by a corona of green and white striped material attached to the ceiling and sweeping out to form graceful folds on each side. The bedspread was covered in a Chinese silk fabric luxuriant with colourful birds and flowers and a small, inviting sofa in one corner of the room with a scattering of cushions repeated the same motif. Other than that, there were spacious mahogany wardrobes, bedside tables, and twin carved chests of drawers. Richard opened a concealed door in one wall, revealing a large bathroom decorated in green and white marble with gold taps.

'There you are,' he said blandly. 'Take as long as you like in the shower and come down and join me for a cup of tea when you're ready. The kitchen is the second door on the right when you come off the stairs.'

Too weary to argue, Emma waited until Richard had left the room, then dropped her handbag on the huge bed, peeled off her clothes and made her way into the bathroom. For five blissful, luxurious minutes she stood under a warm shower, sluicing away all the stickiness of her journey and giving up any effort to think. When she emerged from the bathroom wrapped in a huge, fluffy white towel a practical problem immediately assaulted her. What on earth was she to wear? Hesitantly she pulled open a drawer and was both relieved and annoyed to find that it was full of familiar garments. Her own clothes brought from her house in Rose Bay while she was away in Bali! How had Richard contrived that? He must have phoned Miss Matty and arranged for the clothes to be delivered. But did he honestly think he could simply hijack her entire lifestyle and reshape it to suit himself? Yes, obviously he did!

Smouldering with resentment, Emma pulled on a lightweight green knitted suit and ten minutes later arrived in the kitchen downstairs. There was no sign of Richard, but the air was filled with the fragrance of percolated coffee. Opening another set of French doors, she went out on to a brick-paved terrace and found her quarry. Against the backdrop of the blue, sparkling waters of the harbour Richard was laying a table for two.

'Sit down,' he urged, pulling out a bamboo chair for her. 'I can offer you tea or coffee, Scottish shortbread and Dutch apple cake with cream.'

Emma's eyes widened as she sat down.

'How on earth did you organise all this?' she asked, her annoyance giving way to a reluctant appreciation.

But his reply destroyed all her pleasure.

'I told Amanda to buy the apple cake and cream this morning. She already had the shortbread in the house. She always keeps it here.'

Emma stiffened at this reply. So Amanda was so much at home in Richard's house that she even kept her own food there, was she?

'I thought she was a lawyer, not a general dogsbody,' she remarked tartly.

Richard raised one eyebrow lazily at the snappishness of her tone.

'She is,' he replied. 'And an excellent one. Shrewd, resourceful and always determined to win. But she's also very obliging. She would do anything for me.'

I'll bet she would, thought Emma sourly. Including jumping into bed with you if you simply snapped your fingers. Or has she done that already? A wave of possessive jealousy scorched through her and she gazed at Richard resentfully while he continued cutting the apple cake and fiddling with plates and forks.

'Oh, no cream,' urged Emma as his hand moved to the bowl.

Richard frowned.

'Don't you eat it any more?' he asked. 'You used to love it.'

Emma pulled a face.

'I still do, normally, but I feel rather queasy today. It's probably jet-lag.'

'Probably,' agreed Richard. 'You always did suffer rather from travel sickness, didn't you? Well, why don't you lie down and have a rest after you've finished your tea? I have to go into the office and see Amanda again, so you just make yourself at home.'

As she sat sipping her tea and nibbling her shortbread, Emma's thoughts raced. She couldn't help reflecting on how weird it was. After all, she was his wife, so why should Richard need to urge her to make herself at home? That was something you said to outsiders, to people who didn't belong to a household. Anyone who did belong wouldn't need to be told. But if Richard only saw her as some kind of rather unimportant visitor then why go through with this charade of bringing her back as his wife? Could anyone really want revenge so badly that he would use a woman sexually for three months and then casually dismiss her like an unsatisfactory housekeeper at the end of her contract? She thought of Richard's granite profile on the flight home from Bali and shuddered. Yes, he could. And no doubt the way she had responded to him at Air Panas had simply fuelled his satisfaction with the cruel game he was playing. A hot wave of humiliation flooded through her at the thought of what she had said to him. What a fool she had been, babbling about love! Well, in future she would guard her dignity more fiercely. Abruptly she pushed her plate away, wishing that this ordeal were over. Rising to her feet, she gave Richard a bleak smile.

'Thank you for the tea,' she said firmly, like a child taking her leave at a birthday party. 'I think I'll go upstairs and rest now.'

'Just as you like.'

Fifteen minutes later, lying on one side of the huge king-sized bed, she heard Richard's car accelerating noisily up the driveway. Closing her eyes, she turned her face into the pillow and groaned.

When she awoke several hours later, she found the room filled with the soft apricot glow of the bedside lamps. Richard had just sat down on the bed beside her, making the mattress plunge beneath her, which was what had caused her to wake.

'Are you feeling better now?' he asked. 'I've ordered in some dinner if you're hungry.'

Emma yawned and sat up, pushing her tumbled hair out of her eyes. In spite of her resolve to keep him at arm's length, her heart gave a small, treacherous leap of pleasure at the sight of his concerned face looking down at her.

'Yes, much better, thank you,' she said, blinking. 'I'll come down.'

Before they ate Richard took her on a tour of the house, showing her every detail of its vast, echoing rooms, its Italian chandeliers and ornate plasterwork, its antiquated plumbing and wiring. Emma could not suppress a little thrill of excitement, wishing with all her heart that they really were planning to embark on re-decorating this beautiful old home together. As it was, she felt that she was an outsider who did not belong. So when at last Richard asked her how she liked the place her reply lacked any enthusiasm.

'What do you think of it?' he demanded as they completed their tour of inspection and returned to the kitchen. 'It'll be superb when it's finished, won't it?'

She shrugged.

'I suppose so,' she said indifferently. 'I can't say it appeals much to me right now.'

His face wore an unreadable expression as he looked at her through narrowed blue eyes. But then he seemed to dismiss her opinion as of no account.

'Oh, well, I don't suppose it really matters whether you like it or not,' he remarked. 'Let's go and eat.'

The meal he had ordered was excellent. Roast filleted beef cooked in pastry with a black pepper and mushroom sauce, accompanied by sautéd potatoes and vegetables and followed by a dessert of lemon soufflé. And somehow they managed to skate lightly over the dangerous depths of their relationship, making polite conversation about business matters, overseas holidays they had enjoyed and various plays and concerts that were showing in Sydney. But after drinking their coffee Richard dropped another bombshell.

'By the way,' he said, 'I've invited my mother to lunch on Sunday. I hope that's all right with you?'

Emma's hair almost stood on end at this announcement. She had only met Richard's mother two or three times in the course of their marriage and had always felt that Louise Fielding disapproved of her deeply. But what could she possibly say? She couldn't refuse to admit Richard's mother to his own house, could she?

'Oh, that would be nice,' she said in a failing voice. 'Will she be staying long?'

'Only for lunch and the afternoon. I think it's time you two got to know each other a bit better.'

When Louise Fielding arrived two days later, Emma was still feeling as if she would like to flee the country under a false name. The small, grey-haired woman who was stumping up the front steps with a walking-stick looked just as formidable as ever. But when Emma came to the door to greet her she was unexpectedly touched to find Louise thrusting a bunch of beautiful white Iceberg roses into her hands as she leaned forward and pecked her on the cheek.

'I hope you'll like these, Emma,' she said. 'They're out of my own garden. Richard told me you were very fond of flowers.'

'Thank you,' said Emma. 'That's very sweet of you. Won't you come in and have a glass of sherry?'

Yet in spite of the friendly gesture on Louise's part the conversation over lunch was decidedly strained. Emma, not being a wonderful cook herself, had resorted to using a catering company to produce the meal. The food was very good—thin vegetable soup followed by a savoury chicken and bacon pie with new potatoes and minted peas and an apple crumble for dessert. Yet the conversation was definitely laboured. It was perfectly obvious that Richard hadn't told his mother the truth about their abrupt and unexpected reconciliation. And Louise was doing her best to pretend that the couple had never been apart. Of course this meant that the past eight years of their lives simply vanished into a black hole and was not available for discussion. The result was that Emma and Louise had a very lengthy chat about greenfly on roses while Richard ate his way serenely through the meal, apparently unaware of any tension. But just as they had finished their coffee the phone rang and he rose from the table and went into the hall. Several minutes later he returned.

'That was Amanda,' he announced. 'There's an urgent fax in the office from a shipping company in Singapore which she wants me to attend to immediately. I'll have to leave for an hour or so, I'm afraid. I hope you two can entertain each other.'

He came around the table and kissed them both on the cheek, then left without another word. Emma felt upset at the unexpected interruption. From her own business dealings, she knew that it was all too likely that there was a genuine fax in Richard's office, but why did the wretched Amanda have to help him deal with it? And why did he have to leave Emma alone with his mother who hated her? Suddenly she became aware of Louise's bright brown eyes gazing at her shrewdly in a way that made her feel decidedly flustered.

'More coffee?' she demanded, leaping to her feet.

To her surprise the sudden movement sent an alarming surge of faintness through her. She stood still, swallowing hard as she felt the room swim disconcertingly around her.

Suddenly Louise was on her feet beside her holding her elbow.

'Are you all right, Emma? You've gone quite green. Here, sit down while I get you a glass of water.'

The older woman limped across to the sink, came back with a glass of water and watched while Emma swallowed it.

'Thank you,' said Emma. 'I'm sorry about that. It's just the travelling. It always does make me feel a bit sick, but I'm not usually this bad.'

'What you need is a good rest on the sofa. Go into the little sun-room and have a nap, and later on I'll bring you some tea.'

An hour later, still feeling rather peaky in spite of her rest, Emma accepted a cup of hot, sweet tea and a couple of shortbread fingers from Louise. Somehow this little act of kindness seemed to thaw the atmosphere between them considerably. Louise sat down in a cane chair filled with deep cushions and flashed Emma an unexpected smile.

'I haven't had a chance to say it before,' she murmured, 'but I'm really glad you and Richard are back together.'

'Wh-what?' stammered Emma. 'But you never wanted us to marry in the first place, did you?'

Louise gave a short laugh.

'No, I didn't,' she admitted. 'Although I never had any say in the matter really. You two were already married when I heard about it. And of course that was part of the problem. It hurt my feelings, not being invited to the wedding. Richard did explain to me later that he was afraid I'd try to talk you out of it if I knew what he was planning. And he was probably right, because I certainly would have thought it was a big mistake.'

'Why?' demanded Emma, feeling stunned by this emphatic statement.

Louise picked up her own cup of tea and sipped it.

'Well, in the first place you were too young,' she said in a forthright tone. 'And as for Richard, with all the burdens he already had, the last thing he needed was marriage.'

'What burdens?' demanded Emma. 'What do you mean?'

Louise gave her a startled glance.

'Didn't he ever tell you?' she demanded. Then, as Emma continued to look blank, her mother-in-law gave an exasperated sigh. 'Well, he may be my son, but Richard really is infuriating! Sometimes he's as secretive and strong-willed and obstinate as a mule. Imagine not telling his own wife!'

'Telling me what?' cried Emma.

'Ask him!' retorted Louise cryptically.

'But——' began Emma.

'No, no, Emma, don't cross-examine me about it. Richard's the one who should tell you, although I'm surprised he didn't do so in the beginning. Perhaps if you'd known how much pressure he was under you might have waited longer before you married him. If Richard hadn't been under so much stress and you hadn't been so immature, I'm sure the marriage would have got off to a flying start.'

'I wasn't immature!' protested Emma.

Louise's lips curled in a wry smile.

'Now, don't fly off the handle, Emma,' she urged. 'I don't doubt that you've grown up a lot in the last eight years. The way you handled your father's business after his death shows that. Richard was so proud of you and I had to agree that you did a really fine job with Prero's. But I had good reason to be wary of you in the past. If you hadn't been immature and spoilt, you would never have run off with another man just because you had a silly tiff with Richard.'

Emma's mouth fell open. Was that what Richard had told his mother about their break-up? A burning rush of indignation filled her at the unfairness of it. How could he be so sly, so hypocritical? Whatever faults he might have had in the past, he had never blamed others for his own mistakes and she felt a sharp stab of disappointment at this fresh evidence of his capacity for deceit. Obviously he had twisted the facts to make his mother think that he was squeaky-clean, while Emma was the guilty party. She took a quick, sharp breath to explain, then hesitated. After all, Richard was still her husband, and some odd sense of loyalty made her reluctant to expose him. Instead she simply sighed.

'There was more to it than that,' she said ruefully. And then she thought of her extravagance, her ineptitude in the house, the childish tantrums she had thrown when Richard chose to work rather than spend time with her. 'But I must admit that I made a lot of mistakes. Mind you, Richard wasn't perfect either.'

Louise's brown eyes crinkled in amusement.

'I don't imagine he was,' she replied with spirit. 'He's always been a difficult man to live with. Quick-tempered, obstinate and unforgiving, which is a dreadful combination! But he loves you, Emma, or he wouldn't be back with you, and for the same reason I'm forced to believe that you love him. So I wish you both every happiness.'

This was even worse than the discovery that Richard had twisted the facts to blacken her character. Here was her poor, gullible mother-in-law beaming kindly at her in the naïve belief that everything was well between the supposedly happily married couple. What a joke!

'Thanks,' said Emma bitterly.

Louise began to gather up the tea things with swift, purposeful movements.

'Well, as I said before, I'm glad you're back together. I believe marriage is worth working for and now that you're older and wiser I'm sure that you'll sort all your problems out. And I might add that I don't intend to be one of them, Emma. If I can help in any way I will and you'll always be welcome in my house. Other than that, I'll simply stay out of your affairs and wish you both all the joy in the world.'

Emma flinched.

'That's kind of you,' she said.

'No, it isn't. It's very selfish. I'm longing to be a grandmother and I think you and Richard are my best chance. Besides, during the last year or so I'd really begun to worry that he was going to divorce you and marry that awful woman he's been living with. What's her name, now? Amanda.'

CHAPTER SIX

EMMA had the nightmare sensation that her tongue had frozen in her mouth and that her legs were paralysed. Oh, she had never doubted that there had been other women in the years which she and Richard had spent apart! But Richard would never have lived with anyone else unless he was very seriously involved...and that hurt. In fact, it hurt so much that for a moment she simply sat motionless, feeling chilled and stricken. Before she could move, the door suddenly opened and Richard entered the room. His lazy smile vanished as he caught sight of her face. In two strides he was across the room and kneeling beside her, taking her hand.

'What's wrong with you?' he asked in a sharp voice.

Louise snorted.

'Been working far too hard and far too long if you ask me!' she said. 'She had quite a nasty dizzy turn while you were gone and she doesn't look well to me now. If you take my advice, Richard, you'll send her to the doctor for a thorough check-up. And for heaven's sake make her get some rest and relaxation. I'll be off now that you're home. No, don't get up, I'll see myself out. Goodbye, Emma; I hope you're feeling better next time I see you.'

As the door closed behind his mother, Richard gazed searchingly into Emma's face and frowned.

'Are you ill?' he demanded.

Emma shook her head. She felt as disorientated as if she had just hurtled over Niagara Falls in a wooden barrel, but she didn't believe she was actually sick. What

107

she did feel was a sense of betrayal so acute that she wanted to burst into tears and run away. How stupid! How childish! And what a triumph for Richard, if he only knew how much he had the power to hurt her...

'No, I'm just tired,' she said in a matter-of-fact voice.

Richard rose from his squatting position and sat on the couch beside her, his long legs extended.

'You work too hard,' he reproved her. 'Miss Matty told me that you often go for sixteen or eighteen hours a day.'

'So do you,' retorted Emma.

Richard shook his head gravely.

'I used to, but not any more,' he replied. 'I've no intention of being dead from a heart attack before I'm forty, so these days I delegate a lot of my work. And so should you, starting tomorrow. I'll take you into the new office block so you can see what progress we've made moving in, and we'll organise a new secretary to help Miss Matty. What else? Oh, you'll need someone to inspect the new building sites—I know just the man for you. A fellow called Ron Bortolli, a fine tradesman and a hard worker, as honest as the day is long. Apart from that, you could really do with more help on the legal side of things. Amanda——'

'I don't want Amanda's help!' blazed Emma.

Richard looked at her strangely, his blue eyes narrowing and his lips taking on a pursed, thoughtful expression.

'I was only going to say that Amanda could recommend someone,' he commented mildly.

'I don't want her recommendations either,' snapped Emma.

Richard gripped her shoulders and twisted her round to face him.

'What is this all about?' he said quietly.

Emma was silent for a moment, pressing her lips together. But to her annoyance, when she did speak, her voice was unmistakably wobbly.

'Louise said you were living with Amanda.'

Richard gave a faint shrug that might have indicated amusement.

'That's right,' he agreed. 'What of it?'

Emma's self-control vanished.

'How can you?' she choked. 'I'm supposed to be your wife and you're calmly sitting here telling me that you've been living with another woman! Did you ever think about my feelings? Or hers?'

Richard's rugged features took on a long-suffering expression, as if he were a patient man tirelessly enduring the unreasonable whims of women.

'You're making a mountain out of a molehill, Emma,' he announced. 'You know perfectly well that there's a small housekeeper's flat at the back of this house. Well, Amanda simply stayed there for a few weeks just after I moved here. She had sold her own home and had nowhere else to go until she could get into her new place. But as usual my mother has put two and two together and made five out of it.'

Emma eyed him suspiciously. It sounded like a reasonable explanation, but could she trust him? After all, Louise's other revelations today had shown that Richard could be very adroit at twisting the truth when it suited him.

'She said you were likely to marry Amanda,' she blurted out.

In some subtle way Richard's expression changed. For a moment he looked calculating and then unmistakably shifty.

'It's possible that I might,' he agreed.

Emma gasped. How could he sit there so calm, so mocking and tell her such a thing?

'You callous swine,' she breathed.

'Do you mean you really care?' he asked incredulously. 'Are you still claiming that you love me as you so charmingly told me in Bali? And do you really think I'm gullible enough to believe it?'

The scorn in his voice was so blistering that Emma flinched. Suddenly her misery was swept away in a torrent of hot, vengeful anger.

'No, I'm not!' she retorted with biting sarcasm. 'As you said, telling someone you love him is just part of the sexual game, but it is only a game. What we're talking about here is something else. It's... it's a question of pride! Love doesn't come into it.'

Richard's massive hands tightened so violently on the back of the Windsor chair that for a moment Emma thought the slender slats of wood would snap under the pressure. His blue eyes were narrowed murderously and his teeth were gritted so hard that a muscle was twitching furiously in his cheek. Even the scent that came off him was a hot, primitive blend of leather and soap and raw, enraged masculinity. Instinctively Emma shrank back into the couch, half afraid that she had gone too far in provoking him. Would he take his revenge by wrestling her down into the cushions and showing her in the most blatant way that he still regarded her as his woman, his property? Her heart gave a skip of apprehension at the prospect and yet she was appalled to find a hot, pulsating excitement flooding through her veins as Richard continued to glare down at her. When he gave the chair a violent shove and strode across the room, she felt almost disappointed. Wheeling around like a charging bull, he vented his rage in words.

'So we have the truth at last,' he said in a low, menacing voice. 'We're back together as man and wife, but love doesn't come into it for you. Well, it doesn't for me either, Emma, and since we're not in love with each other it's no concern of yours what I do after we part again, nor with whom I do it. All you need worry about is being a proper wife to me in the short period remaining to you.'

'"Proper wife"?' echoed Emma. 'What's that supposed to mean?'

He scowled at her.

'That you give me what I want. Passionate sex. Total fidelity. And a proper respect for me as your husband.'

Emma leapt to her feet.

'Where did you get your law degree?' she jeered. 'Neanderthal college?'

He crossed the room in two strides and seized her wrist in a grip that hurt.

'I'm not joking, Emma!' he growled, thrusting his face down to hers. 'You can call me primitive if you like, but there are some things that never change between a man and a woman. And one is that any red-blooded man wants his wife exclusively to himself. You ran away from me eight years ago because you preferred another man and I've never forgiven you for it. Well, this time I'm the one with the upper hand and I don't intend to forfeit it. You've come back to me whether you like it or not and, by heaven, you'd better understand that you're back on my terms. And that doesn't include jumping into bed with anybody else. Do I make myself clear?'

'Perfectly clear,' retorted Emma. 'But aren't you being rather hypocritical?'

Richard frowned.

'Hypocritical? In what way?'

Emma twisted out of his grip and flounced across the room. Even now the thought of Richard and Amanda together filled her with such turmoil that it was several seconds before she could speak. She stood fighting for breath until some semblance of calm returned to her.

Then she turned around and looked at Richard with cold, accusing eyes.

'It's perfectly OK for you and Amanda, is it?' she challenged. 'You can go to bed with her, live with her, even tell me you're going to marry her and that's all right! I'm supposed to bite my tongue and look the other way, be the good little doormat while you do exactly as you please. Never mind about love, Richard, never mind about fidelity! What about showing a proper respect for me as your wife? Did it ever occur to you that perhaps any red-blooded woman wants her husband exclusively to herself?'

Richard's rugged features creased into a mocking smile that made Emma long to slap his face.

'So you're beginning to get some idea of the pain and humiliation involved, are you, sweetheart?' he taunted. 'I'm glad to see it.'

Emma caught her breath.

'Oh, go to hell!' she shouted. 'You're such a bastard, Richard! You enjoy tormenting me, don't you?'

'Perhaps,' he agreed with that same cool, indifferent smile.

She took a long, shuddering breath and tried to match his cold, indifferent stare with her own.

'Are you sleeping with her?' she demanded bluntly.

Richard shrugged, his blue eyes narrowed in amusement as they rested on her.

'Maybe I am, maybe I'm not,' he replied. 'Try living with suspicion and doubt for a while, Emma. See how you like it.'

'You don't care about me one scrap, do you?'

'No, I don't,' replied Richard brutally. 'And I'm not going to be a caged tiger jumping through hoops for you, Emma. This time if anyone is cracking the whip it'll be me, so may I remind you that this reunion is not about love? It's about sex, passion, revenge.'

Emma's explosive temper blazed up and with an incoherent cry she launched herself at Richard, intending to slap his face.

'I hate you! I hate you!' she shouted.

But before she could reach him something strange happened. The ground seemed to lurch up to meet her and the room dissolved into a hectic pattern of grey dots. When at last the dizzy, whirling feeling subsided she became dimly aware that she was sitting on the sofa again with her head between her knees and Richard's arm around her. She heard his voice, rapid, anxious, full of concern but strangely muffled so that she couldn't distinguish the words, until at last the ringing in her ears subsided and the floor steadied beneath her feet.

'Emma?'

'Mmm?' She raised her head groggily and blinked at him.

'Are you feeling better now?' he repeated.

She nodded uncertainly and his arm tightened protectively around her shoulders.

'I'm sorry if I brought this on,' he muttered. 'Upsetting you like that——'

'It wasn't that, Richard,' she protested, shaking her head. 'I'm sure it wasn't. I've been feeling awful ever since we left Bali.'

'Stress and overwork,' he retorted. 'But it's stopping right now. Do you hear me? You're going to a doctor tomorrow and after that you're taking a long holiday.'

'Whatever you say,' muttered Emma feebly.

'Hell! Now I know you really are sick.'

Without warning he suddenly rose to his feet and in a single swift movement scooped her off the couch and into his arms. Taken by surprise, she glanced up at his face and saw an urgent, hungry look in his eyes. For a moment she thought it was tenderness, then it vanished abruptly. All the same there was a dangerous potent sweetness in being held so tightly against him. She could feel the warmth of his body coming off in waves, hear the deep, slow thudding of his heart, smell the indescribable masculine scent that reminded her somehow of woodsmoke or leather. In spite of her earlier annoyance she gave him a small, uncertain smile and was shocked when he uttered a low groan and crushed her even more tightly against him. She could not deny that there was an aching pleasure in letting him carry her upstairs to bed. By now she was probably well enough to walk, but it gave her an unexpected thrill to feel his powerful arms about her and to sense the muscular strength of his thighs as he loped effortlessly up the stairs. At last he set her down in the centre of the huge bed and sprawled beside her, gently stroking her long black hair away from her face. Her fainting attack had completely changed the atmosphere between them. In place of the brooding antagonism he had shown before, Richard was now gazing at her with a tenderness that disarmed her.

'Can I get you anything?' he asked. 'Something to eat or drink?'

She shook her head.

'Do you want me to call a doctor?'

Again she shook her head, feeling slightly embarrassed now.

'No, honestly,' she protested, hauling herself up against the pillows. 'I'm fine now. I don't know what came over me.'

'I told you. Stress and overwork. You're going to slow down now, madam. OK?'

Emma gave a soft, rippling laugh.

'Yes, master,' she said meekly.

Richard scowled ferociously at her. 'Are you making fun of me?' he demanded in a threatening tone.

'Of course I am.'

His lips twitched. Abstractedly he twined her long hair around his fingers and raised a lock of it to his lips.

'All the same, it's no joke,' he warned. 'Working so hard, never having any relaxation, never being able to share your problems can just about destroy your life. I know. I've been through it.'

His words woke an answering echo in the back of Emma's mind. She stared thoughtfully at him with her head tilted on one side.

'Your mother said something like that,' she remarked pensively. 'That you were under a lot of pressure and had a lot of burdens when we were first married. What did she mean, Richard?'

Richard released his hold on her hair and drew back, looking suddenly wary and suspicious.

'Nothing important,' he muttered.

Emma leaned forward and grabbed his hand.

'Tell me,' she insisted. 'Don't you think I have a right to know? Especially if that was part of the reason we were always fighting, why we finally split up.'

'I don't know why my mother couldn't keep her mouth shut,' he said in exasperation. 'It was no big deal, really. But, yes, I suppose you could say I was under a lot of strain when I married you.'

'Why?' asked Emma softly.

'It's a pretty complicated story, but the essence of it is this. You know my mother injured her hip in a car accident and that's why she walks with a limp?'

Emma nodded.

'Yes, you told me that. And your father was killed in the same accident, wasn't he? That must have been hard on you, Richard, I can see that. But it happened ten years before you met me, didn't it? When you were sixteen?'

'Yes, it did, but I never really told you the whole story before. You see, what none of us ever suspected was that my father was a compulsive gambler. For years he'd been embezzling money from the firm of solicitors where he worked to pay for his gambling habit. Guilt and fear that he'd be discovered also led him into drinking fairly heavily and that was what caused the accident. When he was killed, the senior partner in the firm discovered everything and told my aunt. She was Dad's sister, but basically she washed her hands of the whole mess. Her solution was that everything my father owned should be sold to help to pay the debts and that the three of us kids should be put in foster homes. Christina was only twelve and John was eight and I knew it would break my mother's heart if that happened. For months she was too sick to be told the truth, but I tackled the senior partner in the firm myself and brought my aunt in to join the discussion. We came to an unofficial arrangement and everything was hushed up.'

'What kind of unofficial arrangement?' demanded Emma.

'Well, there were two things that I vowed to do. The first was to keep the family together. That was relatively easy. I bullied my aunt into telling the child welfare people that she would provide a home for the three of us, but in fact she did nothing of the kind. I was the one who did it. I left school, got a job as a brick-layer on a building site, rented a house and did the best I could for John and Christina until my mother was well enough to come home.'

'How long did that take?'

'Two years, although even then she needed a private nurse for quite a long time.'

'Two years!' echoed Emma. 'And you said it was relatively easy! What was the second thing you vowed to do?'

'To repay all the money my father had misappropriated. That was a lot harder. Everything he had left in his will had to be sold and there were still massive debts. By the time I met you, things had improved a lot, but I was still trying to pay off the last of what was owing. Apart from that, I had Christina studying medicine and John in his last year of an expensive private school. It was a difficult time.'

Emma stared at him.

'Richard, why didn't you ever tell me?' she breathed.

His face still wore a shuttered, defensive look.

'I wanted to protect you,' he said curtly. 'I thought it was my job to provide for you, not worry you with debts and commitments. And I should have been tough enough and ugly enough to handle it on my own. What right did I have to marry you otherwise? You'd always been brought up in the lap of luxury. I wanted to shelter you, cherish you, defend you.'

Emma pulled a face.

'How strange,' she said with a catch in her voice. 'I always thought you wanted to scowl at me and shout at me and make violent love to me.'

Richard cast her a smouldering glance, but his lips twitched.

'That too,' he admitted.

Impulsively she squeezed his hand.

'It was silly, Richard,' she protested. 'I admire you enormously for what you did, but you should have opened up to me about your problems. I know we wouldn't have fought so much if you had. And I certainly wouldn't have been so extravagant or complained so much when you went out and worked overtime. But I wasn't a mind-reader. How could I possibly know what troubles you were going through? You were so moody and irritable sometimes, I used to think that you were regretting that you'd married me.'

'Don't be ridiculous,' snapped Richard. 'I was just racking my brains about whether I could ever repay my father's debts and give you the kind of life I wanted you to have. I never regretted marrying you!'

'Never?' asked Emma huskily.

Richard's face hardened and his eyes held the flickering grey light of a stormy sea.

'Not until you ran off with good old Nigel,' he said savagely.

Emma closed her eyes briefly and shuddered. Why, why did he always come back to that? And why was it so different from his squalid little affair with another woman? Did he seriously think infidelity was all right for men but not for women?

For a moment she was tempted to blurt out the real truth—that she had never slept with Nigel, although she had deliberately let Richard believe that she had. Deceiving him had been a way of hitting back, of showing him that she couldn't care two hoots about his infidelities. Even now she wasn't prepared to sacrifice that tactical advantage. Tell Richard that she had never made love with anyone but him, when all the time he might be planning to leave her for Amanda? Not likely! All the same, she didn't want this bitterness to go on festering between them...

'Don't go on and on about it,' she begged, opening her eyes. 'I can't stand any of it! It was years ago, Richard. And it wasn't the only thing that was wrong between us, not by a long shot. Do you have to go on hating me forever? Can't you just be nice to me?'

Richard's hand crushed her fingers and he stared at her with an odd, brooding look. But at last he sighed and shook his head.

'I don't know,' he admitted honestly. 'But I suppose I could try.'

'Then will you release me from this bargain?' asked Emma in a rush.

Her pride told her that she must make the demand and make it quickly, while Richard's defences were down. Yet the mere act of uttering the words gave her such a stab of regret that she wondered belatedly whether it really was what she wanted. Would it make her happy if Richard agreed to let her go? As it happened, she never had the chance to find out, for a familiar look of stony obstinacy came into Richard's face and he shook his head.

'No, Emma,' he said implacably. 'You're mine and I won't let you go until I choose.'

Her heart gave a treacherous skip of relief at these words, followed immediately by a flutter of apprehension. What about when he did choose to release her? Would he still send her off at the end of the three months? Replace her with Amanda? Her eyes went dark with foreboding at the thought. Putting out the back of her hand, she rubbed his cheek.

'Then can't you at least be nice to me for the rest of our time together?' she pleaded. 'I can't bear to go on the way we are, with all this anger and hatred between us.'

He caught her fingers in his hand and drew them across to his mouth, nuzzling them so that his warm breath tickled her knuckles.

'Why do I feel as if I'm being enticed into a scented trap?' he growled, half to himself. 'All right, you little siren. I'll be nice to you. But don't count on it lasting.'

She put up her other hand so that she was framing his face and could stare straight into his blue eyes. An unexpected rush of affection surged through her. Oh, God, how she loved him in spite of everything! Even now she would welcome him back in a moment if only he would cancel out the past and promise to be faithful to her forever. She gave him a twisted smile.

'I don't count on anything these days,' she said.

For a moment he seemed on the point of saying something, then he appeared to change his mind. Burying his face in her neck, he held her tightly for a moment and then straightened up.

'I think you ought to try and get some sleep,' he said. 'I'll go into the other room so that I don't disturb you.'

A dark, soothing oblivion descended on her and she did not stir for hours. When at last she woke to the touch of Richard's hand on her shoulder, it was early morning. Blinking, she hauled herself up on the pillows and squinted at the sunshine streaming through the window, and then at the hands of the clock on the chest of drawers. Ten past seven! A lazy trail of vapour from the bedside table made her realise that Richard had brought her an early morning cup of tea and she felt strangely touched by this gesture. He was already dressed in a lightweight grey business suit, white shirt and a blue and grey tie and his manner was as pleasant and unruffled as if they had been happily married for the last eight or nine years. Neither of them referred to the previous evening and Emma gave him a puzzled, uncertain smile before reaching for her wrap.

'I'll just dash into the bathroom,' she explained.

When she returned, she was conscious of a feeling of disappointment that he was no longer there, but, climbing back into bed, she took the first reviving sips of tea. It was Earl Grey, weak, black and hot, exactly as she liked it, and she had just settled back into the pillows with a contented sigh, when the door opened and Richard returned. He carried a tray, laden with toast and marmalade, which he set down on her legs before perching on the foot of the bed himself. But before long he was energetically raiding her plate and in the end he ate most of the toast. Emma began to giggle and couldn't stop.

'What is it?' he demanded with a frown.

'You always used to do that,' she complained. 'Bring me breakfast in bed and then eat it yourself!'

He looked guilty and put back the slice of toast he had just purloined, but impulsively Emma reached out and touched his arm.

'No, don't stop,' she urged. 'I like you doing it.'

Their eyes met. In the old days he would have laid down the toast and taken her in his arms. Even now the impulse was there in the sudden flash of warmth and humour that lit his face. There was no trace of the antagonism that had marred the previous evening and suddenly it reminded Emma of a story she had once heard about the trenches in World War One, when Christmas arrived and the soldiers laid down their arms and exchanged gifts in a brief truce. A smile touched the corners of her mouth.

'What are you thinking?' he asked.

She told him.

'Are we at war?' he asked sombrely, reaching up one hand to cup her cheek.

An intense confusion swept over her as she gazed at him and she realised that it was an impossible question to answer. Now that she understood the reason for his short temper early in their marriage, she felt a rush of compassion and sympathy for him. Besides, she was touched by his gentleness when she had been sick the previous evening. Yet at the same time she felt aggrieved by his ruthless, arrogant insistence that he had a perfect right to sleep with other women, while she had to remain a model of wifely fidelity. The image of Amanda, glamorous, efficient and unbearably threatening, rose before her and her green eyes flashed.

'Aren't we?' she countered.

He did not reply, but rose to his feet and paced around the room, and when he spoke he changed the subject.

'Do you want me to make a doctor's appointment for you?' he demanded.

'I honestly don't think there's any need. It was probably just exhaustion that made me dizzy. I feel fine this morning.'

Richard frowned sceptically.

'All right,' he agreed at last. 'I'll leave it at that, provided you promise me you'll go to the doctor if you feel sick again. And that you'll take a good long rest from work.'

'But your move into the Prero's building——' began Emma.

'Is already under control. You're welcome to come in and see what's happening, but I won't have you working long hours in there. What you need is to take time off, have some fun, develop a life of your own for a change. Is that clear?'

Emma rolled her eyes.

'Yes!' she retorted.

'Good. Well, if you'll stop being such a worrywart about the damned business, I'll take you in this morning and you can satisfy yourself that everything is going smoothly. But only for a couple of hours. After that I want you to rest.'

Emma found it remarkably pleasant to lean back in the plush upholstery of Richard's BMW, instead of fighting the early morning traffic herself. Yet when at last the car pulled to a halt in the underground car park beneath her huge new office complex in the central business district she felt a sharp pang of apprehension. How on earth could she face the stares and whispers of her staff when she appeared at Richard's side as his wife? Even worse, what would Richard's employees think of their startling reunion?

But she need not have worried. As they stepped into the immaculate grey- and peach-coloured interior of the lower ground floor, a couple of busy-looking office workers on their way to the lift made way for them courteously.

'Good morning, Mr Fielding, Mrs Fielding.'

It was polite, friendly, but as casual as if this were all part of the usual morning routine. Had Richard briefed his staff beforehand to prepare them for this? Or were they hand-picked for their discretion? Emma flinched, dropping her eyes to the velvety grey carpet so that she didn't have to wonder whether the three men in business suits opposite were casting her speculative glances. Rather to her surprise Richard slipped his arm through hers in a casually affectionate gesture.

'As you can see from the signs on the directory,' he said, gesturing to the left of the control panel, 'my firm has taken over most of the building now, though we've left Prero's in place on the top floor. After I've taken you to meet some of my directors, you can slip up and have a cup of tea with Miss Matty.'

The next couple of hours passed quite quickly for Emma, and she found herself genuinely interested in learning about the details of the many building projects that Richard's firm had tackled over the past eight years. Therè had been an award-winning urban infill housing programme for low-income earners, a seaside tourist development on the north coast, an old people's housing estate that combined medical services and home health with independent living. And many others. More and more she realised that Richard was not only a shrewd businessman, a skilled tradesman and an expert lawyer, but also a compassionate man in touch with ordinary people's needs.

When Richard was called away to the telephone, his office manager continued to describe the firm's many achievements. A glow of pride flared up inside her as the man talked, but it was swiftly followed by a chill sense of disappointment. What right did she have to feel proud of Richard? He wasn't really her husband any more in anything but name and she had played no part in his successes. This whole situation was nothing but a mockery and a farce! She was still flicking through the photo albums with a grim expression on her face when Richard reappeared at her side.

'Well, are you ready to come and have tea with Miss Matty?' he asked. 'It certainly doesn't look as if you're enjoying yourself here.'

She found her father's old secretary, Miss Matilda Pearce, on her hands and knees in a huge office on the top floor of the building, amid a sea of indescribable chaos. Filing cabinets and cupboards were open, papers were dumped all over the floor and Miss Matty was crawling around on the floor like a dressmaker who had dropped a tin of pins. Emma stared affectionately at that ample rear, clad in a viscose navy skirt, and then hurried across to haul the older woman to her feet.

'Emma!' cried Miss Matty, lurching upright and patting distractedly at her grey permed hair and her double string of pearls which hung askew over her tailored white blouse. 'What on earth are you doing here?'

Emma gave a small fizz of laughter.

'I work here, remember!' she replied, kissing the elderly secretary on one flushed pink cheek. 'Now, is there any chance of a cup of tea or not?'

'Of course, my dear, if only I could find the kettle,' replied Miss Matty, gazing distractedly around her. 'What about you, Mr Fielding?'

Richard grinned.

'No, I've got business to attend to downstairs, so I'll just leave you two to catch up.'

Miss Matty gazed after Richard with an oddly furtive expression as the door closed behind him. In fact, she even tiptoed over to the door and opened it again, to make sure he had really left.

'What are you doing?' demanded Emma, vastly amused by this cloak-and-dagger secrecy.

'Oh, my dear girl,' replied Miss Matty remorsefully, sinking into an office chair. 'You can't imagine how guilty I feel about this whole affair.'

'What affair?' demanded Emma, in bewilderment.

'Telling Mr Fielding where he could find you in Bali,' explained Miss Matty, with the guilty air of a spy admitting to the betrayal of state secrets. 'All these years I've worked in this office and never revealed a confidence before. I was afraid you'd be very angry with me, but Mr Fielding's a very determined man when he wants his own way.'

'I know he is,' agreed Emma with feeling. 'And I don't blame you, Matty. Look, here's the kettle under this pile of old Prero's calendars from last year. Do you want me to plug it in somewhere?'

'If you would, dear,' agreed Miss Matty. 'And there are cups in the cupboard over there. Now do sit down and we'll have a nice little chat.'

Emma looked around, but found that the office chairs except for the one Miss Matty was occupying were covered in piles of junk, so she sprang nimbly up on top of a desk and sat with her feet dangling. Miss Matty's rather severe features creased into an indulgent smile.

'You always used to do that when you were little,' she said with a nostalgic sigh. 'Remember how often I ticked you off about it?'

Emma grinned.

'You never meant it, though,' she said. 'You always used to give me a Mars Bar afterwards.'

Miss Matty's brown eyes twinkled. Reaching into the top drawer of the desk, she drew out a brown-wrapped chocolate bar and handed it to Emma.

'There you are,' she said. 'Enjoy it; it may be the last one.'

Emma's eyes widened.

'But why?' she demanded.

'I'm leaving,' explained Miss Matty. 'That's why I'm sorting out all these old files. Mr Fielding has persuaded me to take an early retirement.'

'Do you mean he's pushed you out?' demanded Emma indignantly.

Miss Matty clicked her tongue.

'No, no,' she said soothingly. 'Nothing like that. To tell you the truth, I've been wanting to go for a long time, but I didn't want to leave you in the lurch, Emma, when times were so hard. Now Mr Fielding has assured me that he'll take care of everything, and he's offered me a very handsome redundancy package too. Oh, Emma, I'm so pleased to see you back together again, and not just because of my own advantage either. I know your marriage has had its problems, but I always believed that Mr Fielding truly cared for you. And it was time somebody did, poor little waif that you were. I never thought it was right, the way Mr Prero took you away from your mother and then kept you so secluded when you were growing up. Heartless, I call it.'

Emma felt as if an abyss was opening up beneath her feet.

'What?' she demanded sharply. 'What do you mean?'

Miss Matty sighed.

'Oh, that dreadful custody case, when your father took you away with him, and the way he made it so difficult for her to visit you afterwards. He could be a very hard man, Mr Prero.'

Emma felt as shocked as if someone had just punched her in the stomach. Custody case? Nobody had ever told her anything about that.

'Y-you mean my mother wanted to keep me?' she stammered.

'Well, of course she did, dear. But your father fought her tooth and nail over it and he had the money to win. Very cruel, it seemed to me.'

'I thought you worshipped him,' she faltered.

'Oh, no,' retorted Miss Matty, with a firm shake of her grey head. 'He always paid me a generous salary, but that didn't mean I approved of everything he did. And Mr Prero could be very unpleasant if you crossed him, very vindictive.'

'All these years I've known you, Miss Matty, you've never said anything like this!' exclaimed Emma.

'No. And I shouldn't be saying it now. I always took pride in my discretion, but now that I'm leaving the company I suppose that makes me feel a bit freer. Plus the fact that I've always thought of you more as a favourite niece than an employer, especially when you look like that, with a blob of chocolate on your cheek. Here, let me wipe it off with my hanky, you dreadful girl. Whatever will Mr Fielding say?'

'Say to what?' demanded a deep, masculine voice.

They both spun around with a gasp, then Miss Matty gave a hoarse chuckle.

'To the sight of your wife behaving like a hoyden, swinging her legs, and painting her face with chocolate,' she replied.

Richard chuckled too.

'Mr Fielding will offer to take her to the zoo where she belongs,' he said.

Emma stuck out an extremely chocolatey tongue at him.

'Don't be ridiculous,' she said.

'I'm serious,' retorted Richard. 'You need more rest and relaxation and, as it happens, I don't have a very busy schedule today. After you've drunk your tea, I think we should stroll across to Circular Quay and then catch a ferry to the zoo. The fresh air will do you good.'

To Emma's surprise they did exactly that. In the days before their marriage the zoo had actually been one of her favourite haunts, since she had never been allowed to visit it in childhood. Her father had regarded it as smelly, noisy and vulgar, and had consequently declared it off-limits. Emma had always been touched by Richard's willingness to indulge her childish enthusiasm for the place. Now, as the hot sun beat down on the blue waters of the harbour and the bow wave of the ferry rushed past in a creamy, frothing turbulence, she turned to him with a quirky smile.

'Do you remember how you used to bring me out here before we were married?'

'Of course I do,' he said shortly. 'That's why I thought you'd enjoy it.'

When they reached the North Shore of the harbour, Richard hung back to let the noisy crowd of excited children surge ashore and then took Emma's hand as she came off the gangplank. Up above them the sculptured sandstone cliffs rose like a series of giant natural steps into a cluster of dense, olive-green vegetation. The air was hot and fragrant with the scent of eucalyptus trees and the sounds of chirps and roars and whistles was wafted to them on the breeze. Once inside the zoo, Emma forgot all about the sorry state of her marriage in the pleasure of mooning around, gazing at elephants and watching the antics of chimpanzees. It seemed this was an extension of the truce begun that morning, for Richard said nothing at all to upset her, but simply strode along beside her with a faint, amused smile on his face. At last Emma flopped down exhausted on a bench and kicked her shoes off with a sigh of relief. Richard sat down beside her and his lips twitched.

'Well, are you ready to be taken out to lunch and re-
vived now?' he asked. 'I know of a wonderful little oyster
bar on the waterfront at Middle Harbour.'

Emma fanned herself with her map of the zoo and
purred dreamily.

'Sounds great,' she agreed. 'But how do we get there
with no car?'

'I've already thought of that,' replied Richard. 'I told
one of the office boys to drop my car off in the car park
at the top entrance to the zoo. We can leave whenever
you like.'

Less than an hour later they were loading up their
plates at a smorgasbord in a small bistro overlooking
the water at Middle Harbour. Emma frowned thoughtfully as she looked down at wafer-thin orange slices of
smoked salmon, fresh oysters on a bed of ice, wholemeal
rolls, an array of salads and platters of cold fried chicken
and rare roast beef. Normally she loved oysters, but today
for some reason they seemed slithery and revolting. How
peculiar. With a faint shrug she chose smoked salmon
instead, accompanied by a mound of green salad and a
bread roll, and she passed over the chilled chablis in
favour of a glass of lemon mineral water. Richard's eyebrows rose as he followed her back to their table.

'No oysters?' he marvelled. 'I thought you gobbled
up those things like a deep-water dredge.'

Emma pulled a face.

'Not today,' she said firmly.

He sat down opposite her and took an appreciative
gulp of white wine, before attacking the mound of food
on his plate. They were both hungry and had almost
finished their meal before he spoke again.

'Well, how did your chat with Miss Matty go?' he
asked.

'Fine,' said Emma with a smile. 'At first I was afraid
you were pushing her out of the company, but she says

she's really looking forward to retirement. Do you know, Richard, she told me something really strange today?'

'Oh. What's that?' asked Richard, squeezing more lemon on to his oysters.

Emma paused for a moment, thinking how odd it was that she still found it completely natural to confide in Richard when she couldn't have discussed this subject with another living soul.

'She said my father fought my mother for custody of me when they got their divorce.'

'Did he?' asked Richard with a faint frown. 'What's so strange about that?'

'Well, nobody ever told me about it,' explained Emma. 'Somehow I always had the impression that my mother had just abandoned me, that she didn't want me.'

'I see. I don't suppose good old Frank gave you that impression by any chance, did he?'

Emma flared up. 'I think it's hateful the way you always use that sneering tone whenever you talk about my father. You're just trying to blacken his memory, aren't you?'

'No,' said Richard soberly. Then he pressed the bridge of his nose with his thumb and forefinger in a gesture that he used when he was bone-weary. 'I'm not trying to blacken his memory, I'm simply trying to make you see him the way he really was, instead of as the hero you've made him in your imagination. But for heaven's sake forget your father, Emma! We both spent far too much time worrying about him when he was alive. Now that he's dead, can't we just concentrate on each other?'

As he spoke he stretched out his right hand to her in a simple gesture of friendship. His eyebrows quirked above his blue eyes in a familiar, rueful mannerism that sent an unexpected rush of tenderness surging through her. She let her hand settle warily into his and met his gaze. Steadily he looked back at her with those amazing blue eyes and his lips twisted into a faint smile. Her heart began to hammer furiously and with a fractional hesitation she returned his smile. She wished she knew what he was thinking. Once she would have been certain that she did. That sly, sideways grin and the narrowed eyes would have signalled that he was tired of quarrelling and wanted to make peace. Preferably in bed. Now she no longer trusted her instincts about Richard. It might be a genuine peace offer or it might be simply an attempt to throw her off guard so that he could torment her further. She decided to give him the benefit of the doubt. Her smile grew wider and her green-gold eyes were suddenly luminous with joy.

'All right, Richard,' she said softly. 'Let's concentrate on each other.'

The sunlight was slanting in from the west and the shadows of the gum trees were growing long and dark blue when at last they emerged from the bistro. Once the barriers had been breached, they had begun to talk freely and spontaneously, sharing the events of the past eight years. An overwhelming sense of tenderness and intimacy lapped over Emma and, when Richard put his arm casually round her shoulders as they strolled back towards the car, she nestled instinctively against him. Richard gave her an affectionate squeeze and then stopped dead with a keen, alert look on his face like that of a hunting dog scenting game.

'Just a minute,' he urged. 'There's a "For Sale" sign on that big block of land down by the waterfront. I'll only be a moment.'

Rolling her eyes, Emma strode on alone to the car, but then realised she didn't have any keys. Somehow standing still in a hot car park seemed to make her feel peculiar. Very peculiar. She clutched at the door-handle for support as another of those alarming waves of faintness swept over her. Feeling slightly sick, she leaned heavily against the car, only dimly aware of the way the hot metal burnt her palms and of the sunlight sparkling on the blue water below. She took three or four slow deep breaths and the dizziness began to subside. Bafflement spread through her. What was wrong with her? She had never felt like this in her life, these sudden bursts of nausea, the queasiness at the sight of certain foods... and then slowly an incredible suspicion began to form in her mind. That night in Bali at Air Panas, they had taken no precautions... It was too soon to tell for sure, but... could she possibly be pregnant?

CHAPTER SEVEN

THE thought was so strange, so unsettling that Emma felt she was on a rollercoaster ride of unfamiliar emotions. First a soaring sense of excitement and exhilaration, followed by a sickening jolt as a runaway panic and dismay took hold of her. Not until this moment had she realised how desperately she wanted to bear Richard's baby. Yet how could she, with things as they were between them? Even though they had been happy together this afternoon, there were still many festering wounds in their relationship. Old grudges unresolved and unforgiven, a complete lack of trust and deep communication, the nagging worry of Richard's tie with Amanda... But absurdly she wanted his baby more intensely than she had wanted anything apart from Richard himself. Images rose unbidden to her mind of herself leaning back against a pile of pillows with a tiny newborn infant in the crook of her arm, feeding from her breast. And Richard beside her, embracing both of them and smiling proudly down at her. She gritted her teeth as she admitted that the reality might be far different. Herself alone with the baby, while Richard, now free and divorced, took another woman away on a honeymoon.

'Emma, are you all right?'

Richard's voice, harsh with concern, cut into her blurred thoughts. She blinked and caught a glimpse of herself in the side-mirror of the car. Her face seemed to have turned a delicate shade of pale green that exactly matched her dress. Swallowing hard, she forced a smile.

'Just dizzy.'

'You've been overdoing it, you little fool. Come and sit down for a moment.'

His voice was stern, his arm hugely strong and comforting about her as he marched her to a secluded bench in a cool thicket of shrubs overlooking the water. For a moment he did nothing except hold her in his arms. Gradually the ground began to steady under her feet and some warmth crept back into her cheeks.

'That's better,' said Richard with relief. 'What's wrong with you, Emma? You had me really worried.'

She hesitated, on the brink of telling him her suspicions. Perhaps he'd be overjoyed, delighted. He might crush her in his arms, hold her at arm's length to look at her with incredulous pride and then haul her back to him with a triumphant shout. Or he might not. She thought of those hurtful words he had flung at her by the swimming-pool in Bali and winced. No, she couldn't bear it if she told him and he rejected her. Better to wait. Anyway she wasn't certain.

'It's nothing,' she said briskly.

'Well, I want you to see a doctor.'

'Don't boss me, Richard. I will if it happens again.'

'Promise?'

'All right, you panic-monger! I promise.' She was recovering rapidly now and his concern was beginning to make her feel edgy. 'Look, Richard, I'm fine! Honestly. I'll be well enough for the office tomorrow.'

He made a low rumbling sound deep in the back of his throat that was half-amusement, half-exasperation.

'I don't want to bully you, Emma, but you still look pale. Why don't you take some time off, maybe have lunch with your mother tomorrow or do something just for fun?'

Emma paused, considering his suggestion. But, fond as she had become of her mother in the seven years since

her father's death, she didn't want to see her right now.
Jane Prero was entirely too shrewd and too perceptive.
Half an hour alone with her and she would undoubtedly
extract the true story of Emma's reunion with Richard.
Emma flinched at the mere thought. Even the glib lie
that she and Richard were trying to patch up their marriage hadn't gone down well with her mother when she
had phoned her on her return from Bali. 'After eight
years and all the women he's been involved with? I hope
you know what you're doing, Emma...' she'd said. No.
She definitely didn't feel brave enough for lunch with
Jane.

'My mother's very busy at the moment!' she blurted
out.

'Have lunch with a friend, then,' persisted Richard.

'I don't have any friends,' said Emma with a rueful
grin. 'I've been working too hard for the last seven years
to have time for friends.'

Richard scowled thoughtfully.

'Well, what about that girl who used to live next door
to us in Woolloomooloo? You used to get on well with
her. The one with red hair and freckles who was married
to a law student. Nick Somebody.'

'Smithers,' prompted Emma.

'That's right. What was her name, now? Jenny? Jill?
Something like that.'

'Jenny,' said Emma. 'Yes, she was nice. But I've lost
touch with her. Ever since my father died I've been too
busy to breathe, let alone go out with friends.'

Richard shook his head disapprovingly.

'Your life's a mess, Emma. You've traded everything
important for money and power.'

'But it wasn't my choice!' she protested. 'The ball was
thrust into my hands and I just had to keep running.'

'Well, it's got to stop. You have to figure out what
you do want from life. Look, why don't you begin by

doing a few easy things that you like? Sleep in late, start getting the garden in order, try and meet some new people. It would do you good, Emma.'

Much as she resented Richard's interference, Emma had to admit to herself that it was good advice and the following morning she took it. She didn't even wake until nine o'clock, when Richard had already left for work. After a long, leisurely shower, she pulled on jeans and a knit top and ambled yawning down to the kitchen. To her surprise, she found the table neatly set, with fresh croissants, butter, a pot of strawberry jam and coffee in a Thermos. Propped against the Thermos was a note and her heart gave a little skip at the sight of it. Was it a love letter? But no, when she looked it simply said in bold capitals, 'WE HAVE NO MILK.' Emma's lips twitched.

Early in their marriage, Richard had been in the habit of writing her notes about anything she forgot to buy at the supermarket. Hundreds of notes. Notes that confronted her in every nook and cranny of their house. Now, with an expectant smile, she walked to the pantry cupboard and opened the doors. As she had guessed, a note on the cornflakes packet in huge red letters proclaimed that awful fact, 'WE HAVE NO MILK.' Another one exactly the same lurked in the refrigerator, while replicas lay hidden in the bread bin, the linen closet, the crockery cupboard, the cutlery drawer, the underside of the dirty laundry basket, and the centre page of the newspaper. As she sat down to eat her breakfast, Emma began to giggle weakly. She didn't drink milk in her coffee anyway, but Richard did. She remembered a similar incident years before when she had become so enraged by his tactics that she had chased him into the bedroom, taken up a pillow and begun beating him over the head with it. Inevitably, a note had fluttered out of the pillow case which said, 'WE HAVE NO MILK.' And when at last they had ended up wrestling passionately in the middle of the vast bed Emma had looked up to find that the underside of the bedroom light held a similar message. 'WE HAVE NO MILK.' Richard was such an idiot sometimes! However much he infuriated her, he had always been able to make her laugh...

As she sat eating her croissants and drinking her coffee, her thoughts turned again to Jenny Smithers. Yes, Richard was right. It was a pity that she had let the friendship slide. She had always liked Jenny and it was awful to have your life so taken over by work that you had no time for friendships any more. Besides, Jenny was an extremely good listener. Just as she was thinking it, the front doorbell rang and she got up to answer it.

'Talk of the devil!' she exclaimed. 'I was just thinking of you.'

Jenny stood grinning in the doorway, her face still covered with zillions of freckles, her amber eyes gleaming mischievously and her whole body radiating vitality. She looked exactly as Emma remembered her, apart from the fact that she now appeared to be at least seven months pregnant.

'Richard phoned me,' she explained. 'He suggested I come and visit you. Oh, Emma, it's so good to see you again.'

They hugged each other warmly and Emma led Jenny through to the kitchen.

'Would you like a cup of coffee?' she suggested.

'Yes, please. White with one sugar.'

Emma nearly cracked up.

'I'm sorry,' she gasped when at last she was able to speak. 'We don't have any milk.'

Jenny looked at her strangely.

'Then can I have tea? Weak and black?'

Emma brewed a large pot of tea and they sat down together at the kitchen table. At first she had been afraid that the lost years might have created a feeling of awkwardness between them, but to her delight they seemed to have the same easy rapport they had enjoyed several years before when both their husbands were law students. Jenny buttered a croissant lavishly, dribbled a trail of strawberry jam across its cut surface and gazed curiously at Emma.

'I can't believe you and Richard are back together,' she said frankly. 'What happened?'

Emma hesitated. But Jenny looked so friendly, so concerned, so nice that to her amazement the whole truth tumbled out. Halfway through the recital, Emma had to leap up, snatch a box of tissues and mop furiously at her face before she could continue. She was on her third cup of tea and her tenth Kleenex tissue by the time she had told the whole story.

'So, according to you, Richard cooked up this whole reunion just so that he could have his revenge and then abandon you?' demanded Jenny in an outraged voice.

'Mmm,' agreed Emma tragically.

'I don't believe it!'

'It's true. He told me that was all he wanted. Three months of using me and then a divorce.'

Jenny made a rude noise and reached for another croissant.

'It may be what he wants you to believe,' she retorted sceptically. 'He may even believe it himself. But it's not the real truth. It can't be. He was crazy about you, Emma.'

Emma pulled a face.

'"Was" is the operative word,' she sighed. 'Not any more.'

'I'm not so sure,' said Jenny thoughtfully. 'Deep down he's probably still in love with you. But that very fact would make him feel angry and confused and vindictive. After all, you really gave him a kick in the teeth, running off with Nigel Wellings.'

'Is that what Richard told you I did?' demanded Emma indignantly.

'Yes. Isn't it true?'

Emma wriggled uncomfortably.

'Sort of,' she admitted. 'I did have a brief relationship with Nigel, but only because Richard was already being unfaithful to me. I couldn't bear it and wanted to hit back. For a while I tried to convince myself that I could love Nigel, but I soon realised it wasn't true.'

Jenny whistled softly.

'That is a mess. Still, at least it's all over and done with. It's in the past.'

'I wish it were,' said Emma savagely. 'But I'm not even sure that that's true. You see, I've got a horrible feeling that Richard's got another woman on the string right now. A glamorous, efficient lawyer called Amanda Morris. She even lived here for a while before I came back.'

'Oh, hell!' exclaimed Jenny in disgust. 'Emma, you've got to get this sorted out. You can't go on with this sort of misery and suspicion.'

'I know,' replied Emma. 'And it's even worse than you think. I've got a strong suspicion that I'm pregnant.'

She told Jenny about her symptoms: the nausea, the dizziness.

'Low blood-pressure,' said Jenny, nodding authoritatively. 'I had that in the early months too. Oh, Emma, if you're going to have a baby, you must get your life sorted out.'

'But what can I do?'

'What do you want to do?'

Emma was stricken speechless. The question was so simple and yet so hard. What did she want to do?

'Do you still love him?' Jenny asked.

Emma picked up the silly note about the milk and read it through. Her face creased in a brief, wry smile and then contorted. Was it love? The shared jokes, the pride in his achievements, the silent empathy that sometimes bound them together with invisible force, the passionate, frenzied lovemaking? She wasn't sure. Then she thought of how she would feel if Richard left her now. Desolation, grief, a dreary certainty that all the colour and passion in her life would vanish forever. She might hate him for the way he had wronged her, but there was no other man who could steal her heart as Richard had done. Wasn't that love?

'Yes, I do,' she said at last. 'I'm not sure that I want to, but I do.'

'And do you want to keep him as your husband or would you rather give up the struggle and let Amanda have him?'

Emma was shocked by the scorching rush of indignation that filled her at this question. Richard was hers, nobody else's. And no hard-nosed, scheming lawyer was going to take him away from her.

'I want to keep him.'

'Then you've got to confront him. Get him to talk, sort things out. Tell him what you want and listen to what he says. Marriage isn't easy, Emma. All kinds of things that are only little problems can turn into big problems if you don't talk about them. You must discuss them. Sort it all out, deal with the pain.'

Emma sighed and pushed the teapot across the table to Jenny.

'How did you get so wise?' she asked. 'You and Nick must have a wonderful marriage.'

Jenny bit her lip.

'Actually, we don't have any kind of marriage at all,' she said. 'We're not married any more.'

'But the baby...' faltered Emma.

'I'm going to be a single mother. I do have a boy-friend, but I'm not at all sure that I want to marry him, even now. You see, I left Nick three years ago because I thought I hated him, but I was wrong. All we had were little problems which we didn't tackle. And now it's too late, because Nick is married to someone else. So don't let it happen to you, Emma. If you still love Richard, nurture that love, give it a chance.'

When Jenny finally left, Emma sat down on the couch and pressed her fingers to her temples. She knew in her heart that her friend's advice was sound and she yearned to follow it in every way. If only she could break down the barriers and talk, really talk to Richard, she felt their problems would be halfway to being solved, but appre-hension and wounded pride held her back. What if Jenny was wrong? What if Richard really didn't love her any more and was only trying to hurt and humiliate her? Why should she suffer his sarcasm a second time? After all, she had let down her defences once already and told Richard she loved him. Yet what had it brought her? Only a blistering argument and a renewal of all the old accusations and bitterness! It was true that Richard had shown her a casual kindness while she was sick, but he had never apologised for the cruel things he had said to her. Wasn't it up to him to make the next move, to back down, to apologise if he really cared about her? Emma shuddered. Nothing in her experience of men in general or Richard in particular suggested that that was a likely outcome! If anyone was going to break the deadlock, it would probably have to be her. But she couldn't, simply couldn't face another bout of vindictive mudslinging. There must be some other way... What if she tried to show him without any words how much she wanted their marriage to succeed? She could stay cool but friendly, coax him into their old, favourite hobbies and activities...

* * *

At first Emma thought it was working. She let Richard know that his friends would always be welcome in the house and soon the place was humming with social activity. Emma discovered that he liked to mingle with a wide range of people from cabinet ministers through accountants and business people to old friends from his building days. Many of the long, hot summer days were spent at casual barbecues or sailing on the harbour, while at night there were intimate dinners for two at expensive restaurants and dancing in glamorous nightclubs. Richard also encouraged her to make friends of her own and, with Jenny's help, Emma soon found herself in the thick of a circle of intelligent, hospitable, lively women.

Apart from their social life, Richard and Emma had the business and their home to draw them closer. Although he had ordered her to take a long rest from Prero's, Richard had no qualms about bringing work home from the office to discuss with her and they spent several lively evenings in his study arguing animatedly about new projects or future directions for their companies. Besides, restoring the house was a constant source of interest to both of them. It was fun to pore over colour schemes and choose furniture together, especially now that they could afford to buy whatever they liked. Richard even helped her with the restoration of the conservatory and the garden, which were Emma's real sources of delight. In fact, one Sunday afternoon he spent two hours in the garden weeding in order to give her a surprise. He certainly succeeded in doing that. But Emma was so touched that she didn't have the heart to tell him that he had just dug up all the primulas she had planted the day before.

There were other hopeful signs. Old, private jokes had been resurrected. Sayings that had meaning only for the two of them, reminiscences about past disasters, little gestures that seemed full of significance. These days

Richard could well afford expensive restaurants and had no need to take a packed lunch to work. But on one occasion Emma surprised him with a metal box containing all his old favourites—olive bread, wedges of King Island Brie, pastrami, cherry tomatoes and a can of icy cold beer. That night, when Richard came home from work, he said nothing, but presented her with a sheaf of a dozen long-stemmed red roses whose spicy perfume filled the house for days afterwards. And then there were the nights. Breathless, passionate, exhausting sessions where they explored each other's bodies with a tempestuous tenderness that made Emma gasp even to recall it. Of course, it was still disappointing that Richard would not talk to her about his feelings, still would not take the final move to bridge the gap between them, but Emma continued to live in hope. Surely he couldn't really be having an affair with Amanda and then making love to his wife with such stormy intensity, such passion, such sensuality? But if he did still love her, why didn't he simply tell her so?

For several weeks Emma had the exhilarating sensation that she was skating over very thin ice, skimming along like a bird, enchanted by the inexplicable sense of lightness and joy that sustained her. Yet all the while she had a growing sense of foreboding that this carefree escape from reality would soon come to an end, that she must face the need for painful action. For there was an issue which she couldn't ignore much longer and which would soon force her to sort out her marital problems once and for all. By now she was almost certain that she was expecting a baby. All the signs pointed to it. Stress or travelling in the past had never made her three weeks overdue and then there was the nausea, the dizziness, the strange mood swings from sudden elation to equally sudden despair. And at times an unexpected serenity that made her feel she could float through anything, that her problems would all be solved without any action on her part. But at last she could postpone action no longer.

A little more than a month after their return from Bali she took the difficult decision of booking in for a pregnancy test. The mere act of making the appointment seemed to set all her chaotic feelings in motion again. She was exhilarated, terrified, apprehensive. And on the morning of the fateful day her hands were shaking with panic—or excitement?—as she dressed. The result was that she dropped her jewellery case and spilled a cascade of necklaces, rings and bracelets all over the carpet. Richard gave a groan of laughter and shook his head, then, as she stood there motionless, fell to his knees and began to pick them up. His hand closed on a heavy gold bracelet studded with rubies and Emma caught her breath in a sharp gasp. As she stood staring down at him, she felt her entire body go as cold and rigid as if she were turning to stone. How could she ever trust him again with that cruel reminder of the past lying so carelessly in his large, open palm?

'What's wrong?' he asked, intercepting her stricken stare. 'Emma, what's wrong?'

'Don't you know?' she whispered.

'No. Should I?'

She closed her eyes briefly and shuddered.

'I suppose you've forgotten all about that bracelet,' she accused.

He shrugged, clearly mystified.

'I suppose I must have,' he admitted. 'I certainly don't know why you're staring at it as though it's a poisonous snake. Did I give it to you?'

'Not to me. No.'

Richard gave an exasperated sigh.

'Damn the bracelet!' he announced, flinging it into her jewellery box and rising to his feet. 'If I've offended you somehow over it, I'm sorry, but I don't have time for riddles about such trivial rubbish. Are you having lunch with me today or not, Emma?'

Trivial rubbish! Emma's eyes filled with hot, stinging tears and she bit her lip, trying hard to contain her turbulent feelings. That was another thing that made her feel certain she was pregnant. Normally it took a lot to make her cry, but these days she forever seemed to be going to pieces about some stupid thing or other. Although this time she had good reason to feel upset.

'No, I'm not!' she flared. 'I have a doctor's appointment at twelve.'

'Doctor's appointment?' His voice was harsh and there was no mistaking the flare of alarm in his blue eyes. 'I thought you were feeling better.'

'Well, you were wrong.'

Her stormy tone didn't seem to annoy him in the least. Quite the reverse. The look of concern in his face was unmistakable as he stepped towards her and took her in his arms.

'Emma,' he said hoarsely, 'if you're ill, if there's something wrong with you, we should be sharing the problem, not bickering like this. Sweetheart, tell me what's wrong?'

'Sweetheart'. It was years since he had called her that with anything other than sarcasm in his voice. And his face was so tense, so filled with apprehension, with fierce, protective tenderness, that her heart began to hammer violently. Was this the moment she had been waiting for, the moment when they would end their war? A painful, fluttering hope rose inside her and she swallowed hard.

'Richard,' she began. 'I think I'm——'

The telephone rang.

Without taking his eyes off her, Richard moved sideways and snatched the receiver.

'Fielding,' he said curtly.

There was a long torrent of speech from the other end of the line. Richard sighed, scowled, pressed his thumb and forefinger into the bridge of his nose.

'All right, Amanda,' he replied at last. 'I agree that it's urgent. The easements over the property could be a major headache. Tell the vendor——'

Emma's mouth set in an ugly line. Flouncing across to the dressing-table, she sat down and pretended to be absorbed in applying her make-up, although she had to make a conscious attempt to stop gritting her teeth. Damn Amanda! Why did she have to keep telephoning Richard at home? And even if it was only a business call, why couldn't Richard put her off, especially at such an important moment? She dabbed some blusher high on her cheeks, applied her lipstick with unsteady fingers so that it smudged and then scowled at herself horribly. Richard, his telephone call finished, came over and put his hands on her shoulders again.

'There are things we ought to talk about,' he said curtly. 'This doctor's appointment——'

Emma's heart was still hammering violently and for a moment she simply felt tempted to blurt out all that was worrying her. The fact that she loved him, that she wanted a genuine marriage, that she might even now be expecting his baby. But she had too much pride to go around indulging in fits of hysteria when at the end of the day Richard was all too likely to run off with Amanda. If I have nothing else left, vowed Emma grimly, at least I'll hold on to my dignity. Taking a deep, steadying breath, she rose to her feet and shook off Richard's hands.

'Not now!' she said with a calmness she did not feel. 'I want to go into the city and you've got work to do. Don't worry, Richard! It's only a routine check-up.'

Richard offered her a ride into the city, but she preferred to take her own car in order to have more freedom

of movement. By the time she reached the doctor's
surgery at Bondi Beach, she had almost forgotten about
Richard and Amanda amid a haze of incoherent hopes
and fears about the forthcoming pregnancy test. When
at last she was shown into the doctor's office half an
hour late and stammered out her explanation she was
disappointed by his matter-of-fact manner. As he looked
down at the Petri dish in his hand, she could no longer
contain her impatience.

'Well?' she blurted out.

He gave her an amused smile and nodded slowly.

'Congratulations, Mrs Fielding. I think we can safely
book you in for the maternity hospital about the ninth
of November.'

With a squeal of shock and excitement, Emma leapt
up out of her seat and beamed joyfully at the doctor.
Even her apprehension about Richard seemed to have
vanished in a positive tidal wave of euphoria.

'That's wonderful!' she cried.

She still felt as if she was dancing on air as she came
out of the surgery and made her way around to the side-
street where she had parked her car. To her chagrin, she
realised that she must have been so overwrought earlier
on that she had forgotten to put any money in the parking
meter. Inevitably a council meter man was already busy
writing out an infringement ticket for her. A momentary
spark of irritation flared through her and then was gone.
What did it matter anyway, today of all days? She was
pregnant! She was going to have a baby! Beaming hugely,
she made her way up to the parking meter attendant.

'This your car?' he asked.

Emma nodded.

'Sorry, love,' he said, tearing off the ticket and handing
it to her. 'I've already written your registration number
in. Can't change it now.'

'That's all right,' said Emma, still beaming. She flung her arms around him. 'Guess what? I'm going to have a baby!'

The startled council man took a step backwards with an uneasy expression on his face.

'Well, it's not mine!' he said.

Once she was inside her car, Emma began to giggle. He must have thought I was quite mad! she said to herself. Poor man. But I feel mad—in fact I feel delirious with joy! I just couldn't believe this would ever happen to me and now it has. If only Richard were here to share it with me... That thought brought her down to earth with a bump. Richard! What on earth was she going to tell Richard? Starting up the car, she began to drive, but found she could not concentrate. She was tempted to go straight to the Prero's building, burst into Richard's office and tell him the news at once, but common sense restrained her. It wasn't something that she wanted to discuss amid the uproar of an office environment with employees likely to come in at any moment. No. Better to stay calm and wait until he came home. And then they really must try and solve their problems.

It wouldn't be easy, but she was sure it was the right thing to do. Deep in her heart, she knew that she loved Richard and would like nothing better than to be a genuine family with him and the coming child. Then the thought of Amanda rose to torment her and her mouth hardened as if she were negotiating a settlement in a tough business meeting. She could not, would not go on as they were at the moment. If Richard really was involved with Amanda, he must swear to give her up and be faithful to Emma alone. Or this ridiculous farce of a marriage must end immediately. The mere thought of a divorce sent a pain like a knife stabbing through her breast, but she knew it would be better than the lies and deceit, the web of intrigue which seemed to have strangled her marriage from the very beginning. If Richard could not love her and her alone, it was better that she should have a clean break and make a new life alone with her child.

As she drove towards Vaucluse, her natural optimism slowly began to reassert itself. Like a ship battered by the onslaught of too many furious waves, she had been in danger of going under, but now she was slowly regaining her equilibrium. That strange tranquillity was descending on her once again. 'Maternal placidity', the doctor had called it, and told her that it was nature's way of ensuring that expectant mothers didn't worry too much. Well, if anybody needed a strong dose of maternal placidity, Emma certainly did! The thought that Richard might elope with Amanda and leave her and the baby alone was more than she could bear. And yet, deep down, some blind, hopeful instinct told her that she would never have to bear it.

Oh, there were problems between her and Richard, no question of that—problems which would have to be resolved. But when she stopped trying to force her tired brain to think about it all, some primitive certainty whispered in her ear the reassurance that he still loved her. Dozens of images flashed before her mind, repeating the message. Richard bringing her early morning cups of tea, Richard worrying over her health and her gruelling work schedule, Richard making love to her in the glowing lamplight with an expression of hungry longing in his face, Richard quarrelling with her as if he really cared about the outcome. He might tell her that he hated her, he might even believe it himself, but it wasn't true! It could not, must not be true! And somehow she would find a way to reach him again, to rekindle the damped-down fires of love that she passionately believed were still smouldering in his heart.

Somehow she would do it. For her own sake. For her baby.

As she parked the car on the brick patio at the rear of the house and strode indoors, a surge of confidence and affection swept through her. Everything would come right between them, she knew it would! She was surprised to see Richard's BMW parked by the conservatory and realised that he must have come home early from work. Perhaps he had done it for the very same reason that she was here—to hack a pathway through the thorny hedge of problems that had grown up between them, to gather her in his arms and never let her go. She tiptoed into the house, hoping to surprise him, then noticed that the sitting-room door was open. With a mischievous smile, she peeped in.

'Richard?'

Suddenly the smile froze on her face. For on the gold and white sofa sat Amanda Morris with Richard crouched on the floor in front of her, holding both her hands in his. At the sight of Emma he sprang to his feet with a ludicrous expression of dismay on his face. But his momentary alarm and apprehension was soon replaced by an air of arrogant challenge. Shocked beyond measure, Emma took a step forwards.

'What's going on here?' she demanded sharply.

'Nothing,' insisted Richard. 'It's nothing to worry about, Emma.'

'Don't say that!' cried Amanda, jumping to her feet and seizing him by the arms. 'Don't say that I'm nothing! I love you, Richard.'

Emma took a step backwards, shaking her head in a dazed fashion.

'You can't do this to me, Richard!' she said in a voice that wobbled on the edge of hysteria. 'You can't flaunt your mistress at me in my own home. I won't stand for it! Make her leave.'

Richard disengaged Amanda's grip on his arm and looked from one woman to the other with an inscrutable expression. Then he gave the young lawyer a brief, reassuring squeeze on the shoulder.

'You'd better go now, Amanda,' he ordered curtly. 'We'll talk about this later.'

'She's the one you should be telling to leave, not me!' protested Amanda. 'You know you love me more than her, Richard. You do, you do!'

'Amanda!' Richard's voice cut through the room like a whiplash. 'Control yourself. I'll talk to you about my plans when you're calmer. In the meantime, remember I'm counting on you to go to Gosford and handle that property deal. Don't let me down.'

Amanda crossed the room and stood in the doorway, her shoulders heaving.

'I'll never let you down, Richard!' she said in a throbbing voice. Then her face crumpled and she fled from the room.

Richard heaved an exasperated sigh, ran his fingers through his curly hair and took a step towards his wife.

'Emma, I can explain——' he began.

'I'm sick of your threadbare explanations, Richard,' blazed Emma. 'You've just used that unfortunate girl as callously as you've used me. But never again. I don't care what it costs, you can bankrupt me ten times over, but it's finished between us, finished! Do you hear me? Now take your ring and get out of my life!'

With a desperate, wrenching movement she tore off her gold wedding-ring and flung it at him. Then, after uttering a single low, unearthly cry, she ran from the room. Her heart was pounding and she could hear Richard's echoing footsteps in hot pursuit by the time she reached the top of the staircase. Sobbing for breath, she ran the full length of the upstairs corridor, flung herself into the bedroom and slammed the door. With shaking fingers she turned the key in the lock and, careless of her condition, began to drag one of the heavy bedside tables into place beneath the door-handle. Moments later a thunderous knocking began.

'Let me in, Emma, or I swear I'll break this bloody door down!'

'Break it down, then! That's just what you'd enjoy, wouldn't you? Coward, bully, liar, womaniser!'

'Emma, listen to me, damn you! There's a perfectly simple explanation——'

'Sure! If only I were simple enough to believe it. But I'm not any more. I'll never believe another word you say, you bastard! You lying, deceitful, heartless bastard . . .'

A sudden convulsive sob rose in Emma's throat, threatening to choke her. Collapsing on the bed, she howled like an injured child, rocking backwards and forwards, gasping and shuddering for breath.

'Hell, Emma, are you crying? Let me in! Sweetheart, it's all just a stupid mistake! There is nothing for you to cry about, I swear it.'

Even now that husky baritone had the power to weaken her defences. For a moment she almost rose to her feet and unlocked the door, then the memory of her grievances rose again and with a furious movement she thrust out her arm, sending a crystal vase on the bedside table shattering to the floor.

'Emma, what happened? Are you all right?'

His voice was sharp with alarm. The hypocrite, the traitor!

'Yes, I'm all right. No thanks to you,' she said through her teeth.

'Let me in; I can sort this out in two minutes!'

Unable to bear another word of his lying blandishments, she was seized by a sudden inspiration. Shooting to her feet, she ran across the room and grabbed the portable CD player. Then, with trembling fingers, she rifled through Richard's box of CDs. *The Ride of the Valkyrie*—that should shut him up!

It did, but it almost deafened Emma in the process. As the tempestuous flood of Wagner's music thundered into the room at top volume, she stuck her fingers in her ears. Beneath the uproar, she could still hear Richard hammering and shouting at the door, but only an occasional word penetrated the noise.

'Amanda ... love ... stupid ... you ... door ... Gosford ... now...!'

After a long time, she no longer heard anything except the Wagner. Taking her fingers out of her ears, she cautiously lowered the volume on the CD player and listened again. Nothing. She tiptoed across to the door and waited. It might be a trick. Then from outside the house she heard the engine of Richard's BMW being gunned into life. Hastily she ran to the window and looked out just in time to see the car vanishing up the driveway with Richard at the wheel.

Richard! she said soundlessly, her fists raised and her face pressed to the glass.

As she turned away, a feeling of terrible desolation and emptiness gripped her. She had told him to go, but somehow she hadn't believed he would. Deep down she realised now that she had been hoping for a miracle. That he really would produce an explanation so watertight she would have to believe it. Instead, she had exactly what she deserved for being so naïve. He had abandoned her without any explanation at all.

Hours later, when she lay staring into the darkness, her face swollen and blotchy from crying, the phone rang beside her. Feverishly she leapt to answer it. It was him, it must be! He was going to apologise, explain, make everything come right.

But it wasn't Richard's voice on the line, it was Amanda's. Cool, mocking, unmistakably hostile.

'Emma? Amanda here. I've just rung to say that Richard and I are at Gosford together. Don't expect him home any time soon. He's staying with me.'

CHAPTER EIGHT

EMMA acted instinctively to silence that hateful, triumphant voice. Crashing down the telephone receiver, she held it in place as fiercely as if she were squashing a scorpion. Then the thought occurred to her that Amanda might try to ring back. Or, worse still, that Richard might do so. And she no longer had even a faint lingering wish to hear the sort of lying excuses that Richard would invent...'Emma, I can explain... Sweetheart... There is nothing for you to cry about...' Damn him! Snatching up the receiver again, Emma left the phone off the hook. Then, rising to her feet as weakly and shakily as if she had suffered a bad bout of influenza, she stumbled around the bed to the door. The bedside table was still jammed in place under the door-handle and there were fragments of the broken crystal vase all over the floor. With a furious gesture she picked up the bedside lamp and hurled that on the floor for good measure. The crash of breaking porcelain made her feel marginally better. But only marginally.

Swearing under her breath, she marched downstairs, found a dustpan and broom and returned to gather up the fragments of the shattered vase and lamp. A small sliver of crystal pierced one of her fingertips and she watched in wonderment, grimly surprised to discover that she felt no pain. It was as if her capacity for feeling anything had frozen, but she went into the bathroom, washed her finger and put a piece of sticking plaster on it. After that, still moving jerkily like a robot, she took the Wagner CD out of the player and dropped it into the waste-paper basket. Then, picking up her dustpan and brush, she went downstairs to the kitchen. She was tempted simply to go out into the night and walk herself into a state of exhaustion, but something restrained her. You must take care of yourself for the baby's sake, an inner voice whispered. Don't let this destroy you, Emma; you're stronger than you think.

Finally, obedient to that prompting, she boiled some water and made herself a cup of tea. Yet even that simple action seemed to be fraught with dangerous emotional consequences. As the light, steamy fragrance of the Earl Grey rose to her nostrils, she had a vivid flash of memory about Richard bringing her breakfast in bed, and that one image triggered off an army of others. Memories of Richard, a blond giant in a pale grey suit, at their register-office wedding with love and pride shining from his blue eyes. Memories of the powerful embrace of his arms as he carried her across the threshold of their tiny terrace house. In her mind's eye she saw again how he had filled the entire place with flowers. White liliums, creamy frangipani, tubs of pink and white begonias. Even the bed had been hung with garlands, so that her first sexual experience had taken place under a canopy of flowers. Now, remembering it, she closed her eyes and shuddered. He must have loved her once, mustn't he? Even if he had nothing but cruelty and bitterness left for her now, he had loved her when she was his bride! Hadn't he?

Don't think about it Emma! she told herself savagely. That's not what it would be like if you stayed with him now. Even supposing he allows you to stay. The rest of your life won't be a bed of flowers, it will be like this! Exactly the way it was tonight! Suspicion, pain, squalid little discoveries about other women and an ongoing pretence that everything is all right. Is that what you want? Is that really what you want? With a muffled groan she set down her teacup and buried her face in her hands.

'No!' she exclaimed aloud. 'No! I want something better than that. For myself. For my baby.'

How long she sat there she didn't know, but when at last she picked up the tea again and sipped it it tasted cold and bitter. She could hear the night-time noises of the house—the ticking of the grandfather clock in the hall, the rustle of an untrimmed tree beating against the glass of the dining-room window. She had always meant to get that tree pruned, or even dug out. Well, it would be up to Richard to do it now, for she wouldn't be living here for a day longer.

Even now, fool that she was, that thought sent a barb of pain through her. Ever since Richard had come back into her life, some blind, stupid optimism had made her cling to the hope that everything was going to come right between them. That they would resolve their differences, fall passionately in love again, stay in this beautiful old house and raise a family together. How gullible could she be? Well, it was time she started planning her future alone. Her three-month reunion wasn't over, but there was no way she could remain for the rest of the time, no matter what he did to Prero's. There was only one course which her pride would allow her to take now. She must pack her belongings, move out and file for a divorce. There was no other choice.

For the remainder of that night and most of the next morning Emma moved about the house, stormily packing her possessions. It was surprising how much she had accumulated in the few short weeks that she had been living there, but at last the job was done. She was just closing the locks of the last suitcase when she heard the sound of car wheels outside on the drive. In spite of all her good resolutions her heart leapt and then plunged again. Sooner or later she would have to face Richard and it was probably better to get the ordeal over immediately. With her head held high and her jaw jutting at a dangerous angle, she went to the back door. But it was not Richard who stepped out on to the brick patio, it was Amanda.

Dressed in a Prince of Wales checked suit, a white silk shirt and black Italian pumps, she looked as brisk and dangerous as a storm-trooper. Casting Emma a swift assessing glance, the young woman picked up her black leather briefcase and strode confidently towards the door.

'I'd like to talk to you,' she said without any preliminary greeting.

'What about?' demanded Emma coldly.

'About the divorce.'

'What divorce?'

Amanda smiled contemptuously, as if amused by these childish delaying tactics. Her carefully plucked blonde eyebrows rose into sardonic peaks.

'Yours and Richard's of course,' she said sweetly.

Emma caught her breath and stepped back a pace.

'What makes you think we're getting a divorce?' she challenged.

Amanda gave a faint sigh. 'Do you mind if I come inside?' she asked. 'It's a rather delicate matter. I'd like to discuss it somewhere a little more private.'

Feeling as if she were giving ground before an enemy attack, Emma ushered her inside the house and led her into the sitting-room. As if she were preparing for a consultation in her office, Amanda unclasped her briefcase and laid a couple of folders on the coffee-table. Then she uncapped a gold pen and looked up expectantly at Emma.

'Richard has asked me to sound you out on the subject of the divorce,' she said. 'He's prepared to be generous if you're co-operative.'

'What do you mean?' asked Emma, aghast, wondering why Richard couldn't at least have the decency to deal with the matter himself.

Amanda shrugged.

'Well, it's obvious that this trial reconciliation with you hasn't worked out, so Richard wants to end it. If you agree to leave quietly, he'll make sure you get a generous settlement.'

Emma bristled with anger.

'And where do you come into this? Are you acting as his lawyer?'

Amanda swallowed a secretive smile.

'No. Somebody else will handle the court work for the actual divorce case. It wouldn't be ethical for me to do it, since I'm an interested party.'

'"Interested party"?' flared Emma. 'In what way?'

'It's obvious, isn't it? Richard and I have been lovers for over a year; we even lived together for a while. But he was always haunted by his first marriage to you. He told me that he wanted a trial reconciliation with you to make certain that things were really over between you. If they were, he promised he would get a divorce and marry me.'

This glib announcement pierced Emma's heart like the thrust of a dagger. What Amanda was saying was outrageous and yet it tallied with everything Richard had told her. Wasn't it the most likely explanation of his extraordinary decision to bring Emma back for a short trial period?

'I see,' she said evenly, striving to keep her composure. 'And now?'

Amanda smirked.

'Now he's certain. He wants to divorce you and marry me. But he still feels financially responsible for you so he asked me to sound you out about a discreet solution for everybody. If you go overseas now without any fuss and stay away for at least eighteen months, Richard is prepared to offer you a very generous settlement. I can't make any promises, but I imagine it will be in the region of twenty million dollars. I've a first-class round-the-world ticket here, made out in your name. You can go wherever you like—Europe, the United States, it's your choice. Just make sure you stay away for a long time.'

'And if I refuse?' demanded Emma.

With a shrug Amanda put the folders back in her briefcase, leaving the airline ticket on the coffee-table.

'Financially you'll be much worse off if you refuse,' she replied. 'But that's not the point, is it, Emma? The real point is this—if you leave now you'll go with your pride intact. Richard will simply tell everybody that the reconciliation didn't work out and you left him again. But if you stay you'll have to suffer the humiliation of having Richard walk out on you and move in with me. And how will that feel? You'd be wise to think about it and give in gracefully, Emma.'

A blaze of hatred surged through Emma as she stared down at the pert young woman callously telling her that her marriage was over. For a moment she was tempted to slap the mocking smile off Amanda's face, but she clenched her fists and restrained herself.

'Leave my house,' she hissed.

Amanda rose to her feet with a graceful, unhurried movement that showed off her long, elegant legs.

'All right,' she agreed sweetly. 'But I suggest that you leave too. Now. Today. Before Richard moves back in with me and the gossip columnists get wind of what's happening. Think about it, Emma.'

Emma could think about nothing else. She thought about phoning her mother or Jenny or Miss Matty and pouring out all her troubles, but she shrank from the humiliation of revealing that Richard could be such a callous swine. Meanwhile the airline ticket lay on the coffee-table, as unwelcome as a redback spider, drawing her gaze each time she passed it with a hateful, hypnotic magnetism. What should she do? What on earth should she do? She hated the thought of giving in to Amanda's demands. It seemed so cowardly to surrender without a fight! And yet wasn't the battle already lost? Richard had made it clear to her from the very start that their reunion was not a genuine trial reconciliation, that he had no long-term hope of reviving their marriage. All it had been was a callous exercise in power politics on his part. So what would she gain by staying around for further humiliation? Even if she moved back to her own house in another part of Sydney, she was haunted by the certainty that Amanda would carry out her threat—that there would be yet another wave of speculation in the newspapers and the glossy magazines about why her marriage to Richard had failed for a second time. She didn't feel she could bear it. And the image of Bali rose like an inviting sanctuary from all the troubles of the last few weeks... In the end she simply climbed into her car and drove around for several hours, fruitlessly trying to sort out her tangled thoughts and emotions.

When she returned home she was surprised to find a grey limousine at rest in the driveway of the house, with a bored-looking youth of about nineteen leaning against it drumming his fingers on his thigh. At her approach he leapt into action, straightening his tie and walking across towards her.

'Good afternoon, Mrs Fielding,' he said, touching his cap. 'Mr Fielding sent me to remind you that you're attending the crippled children's dinner and ball tonight at the Dunsford House. I'm supposed to drive you there.'

'I'm not coming,' said Emma flatly.

The young man's expression of dismay was immediate and unmistakable.

'Oh, please, Mrs Fielding,' he begged. 'You've got to come. Mr Fielding said he'll fire me if I don't bring you.'

'What?' she demanded in outrage. 'That's ridiculous!'

'It's true!' he exclaimed. 'He means it too. And this is the first job I've had since I left school. I've been unemployed for over two years. Please, Mrs Fielding, just come for a little while.'

That *rotten* schemer. Emma bit back the actual words, but they burnt the back of her throat like battery acid. Trust manipulative old Richard to think of some way to get her to do what he wanted. Well, it wouldn't work; she wasn't going to be swindled like that! Then she looked into the boy's pleading brown eyes.

'You will come, won't you?' he begged.

Emma surrendered.

'All right, I'll come,' she agreed. 'Just wait while I change into my evening dress.'

Fifteen minutes later, her eyes sparkling angrily and her head held high, Emma swept out of the house to the waiting limousine. Determined not to show any sign of weakness, she had dressed carefully in a stunning scarlet chiffon evening dress. Her dark hair was swept up into a gleaming chignon, her make-up was flawless and she wore an ornate gold and ruby necklace with matching earrings and bracelet. As the young driver held open the door for her, he gave her a glance of unmistakable admiration. Leaning back in the deep, cushioned leather seat, she consciously tried to calm her racing pulse and turbulent breathing. Try as she might, she could see no good reason why Richard had summoned her to this ball, unless he saw it as another opportunity to humiliate her. Well, if he did, he was going to have another thought coming! Emma was fed up with appeasement. If a confrontation was brewing, she would welcome the opportunity to tell Richard a few home truths about himself. No longer was she going to be the good, humble little wife, following in her husband's shadow. No! If Richard dared say a word to her tonight, she would let him have the full force of her scorn and then walk off and leave him!

It was nearly eight o'clock when the limousine pulled up outside a beautiful old Georgian house in Elizabeth Bay set in a couple of acres of lush, subtropical garden. Although there was a huge golden moon already rising in the dark blue sky, the gravel driveway was softly lit by yellow coach lamps and the same golden glow from concealed lights bathed the front façade of the house.

As the limousine drew up in front of the main door, Emma leaned forward and spoke to the young driver.

'I want you to wait for me in the side-street next to the house. I may not be staying long.'

'Yes, madam.'

A doorkeeper in a black suit covered with gold braid, black top hat and white gloves helped her out of the car and escorted her to the front hall of the house. Once inside, she handed over her wrap to a cloakroom attendant and looked about her. Although tickets to the dinner and ball cost several hundred dollars per head, the house was already thronged with Sydney socialites. Overhead a massive Italian chandelier hung from an ornate ceiling rose, casting dancing beams of light on the crowd that thronged below. The men were in black dinner suits and the women in brightly coloured evening dresses and they were all talking so energetically that a low drone of conversation like a humming of a hive of bees rose into the air. As Emma stood hesitating on the outskirts, a waiter with a round silver tray glided up to her.

'Champagne, madam?'

'Thank you.'

She took the long-stemmed crystal glass, raised it to her lips and took a swift gulp. The fizzy, sparkling liquid seemed to diffuse instantly into her bloodstream, making her cheeks flush and her head swim. She smiled grimly. There were so many people here that with any luck she wouldn't even have to see Richard. But then some instinct, a prickling sensation between her shoulderblades, made her turn around sharply and there he was. Even at such a moment she felt her heart give an unwelcome leap at the sight of him. Bulldozing his way through the crowd, he was a good five or so inches taller than most of the men present and with his wild, curly blond hair he reminded her of a surfer breasting the waves. Except that no surfer was likely to wear such an ominous scowl. The last remnant of people melted away before him and he appeared in front of her.

'Emma.'

'Richard.'

The very air seemed to crackle with their hostility. His powerful fingers closed on her upper arm and she gave a protesting gasp. Flagrantly ignoring this, he took the champagne glass from her nerveless fingers, deposited it on a polished blackwood table and steered her towards a side-door.

'Where are you going?' she demanded indignantly. 'I've only just arrived. I've——'

He cut her off.

'Outside. Into the garden. I want to speak to you.'

They turned a corner and the scent of expensive perfumes gave way to the warm, delicious kitchen odours of beef and red wine. Then he opened an outer door and she found herself on a brick terrace where a string quartet of musicians was playing a piece by Vivaldi. Still holding her arm in a grip like a vice, Richard hustled her down a set of stairs into a sunken garden where a floodlit fountain played amid a grotto of volcanic rocks.

'Why the hell did you shut me out last night?' he demanded in a voice that was tense with suppressed rage.

Emma gasped angrily.

'Oh, you don't think I had sufficient reason?' she hissed.

'No, I don't. You——'

At that moment the reverberating tones of a brass dinner-gong were heard from inside the house. Seizing her opportunity gladly, Emma wrenched herself free from Richard's grasp, picked up her long skirts in her hands and fled nimbly back up the stairs.

'I'm going in to dinner,' she announced over her shoulder.

Once inside, Richard caught up with her and, for all her fuming, she could not avoid being seated next to him at the meal. In other circumstances, she would have loved the elegant dining-room, with its Regency striped gold and white wallpaper, its vast table set with heavy silver, Waterford crystal and fine Royal Doulton china and the silent, efficient waiters, gliding across the parquet floor. The food and drinks were excellent too. An assortment of Tasmanian seafood, followed by *boeuf en croûte*, new potatoes, mushrooms and courgettes, a raspberry torte, various delicious cheeses, and a subtle selection of fine Australian wines. But Emma might as well have been eating ashes for all the pleasure it gave her. She waved away the oysters, picked at a little asparagus with hollandaise sauce, pushed her beef and vegetables around her plate and refused all offers of pudding or coffee.

'Are you still sick?' demanded Richard curtly.

'No.'

'Then stop acting like a spoilt brat and eat,' he growled under his breath.

Emma flung him a stormy look and said nothing. At the far end of the table on the opposite side she had just realised that Amanda Morris was sitting watching her, looking like an advertisement for aluminium cooking foil in a long, textured dress of silver lamé with matching dangling earrings. For an instant the two women's eyes met and held and Emma felt a suffocating sense of despair rise inside her. She's won, she thought dismally; she's won. Why did Richard ever have to give way to her? Fortunately the last course was now finished and Emma was soon able to leave the table. But the ordeal was not over. There was still the ball to come.

The ballroom at Dunsford House ran the full length of the building and was regarded as a masterpiece of late Georgian colonial architecture, but Emma had no eyes to spare for its graceful proportions or for the ornately upholstered chairs which stood around the walls. The moment they entered the room, the band struck up the first waltz and Richard's hand closed on hers in a hard, hurting grip.

'Would you like to dance, Emma?' he asked in a tone that made it more of an order than a request.

'No, thank you,' said Emma coldly. 'Why don't you ask Amanda?'

Richard's mouth hardened and a stormy light burned in his blue eyes.

'Perhaps I will,' he retorted.

And, turning his back on her, he strode across the room to where Amanda was seated on the opposite side. A moment later they were whirling gracefully round the dance-floor.

Emma didn't wait to see any more. It was quite obvious that Richard had made his choice and there was nothing to be gained by staying around to be humiliated further. Threading her way through the crowd, she broke free into the entrance hall, hurried across to the impromptu cloakroom which was set up in the small front parlour and retrieved her wrap. Then, almost running now, she hurried out on to the front steps of the house and spoke to one of the young doorkeepers who was still on duty outside.

'I have a driver waiting for me in a grey limousine in a side-street just around the corner. Could you ask him to come and fetch me now, please? I want to go home.'

The drive back to Vaucluse was a nightmare. All she could see in her head was the indelible picture of Amanda, clasped in Richard's arms, whirling around the ballroom to the strains of a Strauss waltz. By now Emma was beyond tears, but a mysterious ache seemed to grip her entire body. When the limousine finally drew to a halt at the foot of the drive next to her house, she found that she was thinking and planning like a hunted animal. Pulling a folded fifty-dollar note from her purse, she thrust it into the hand of the young driver.

'I want you to park in the shadows behind the conservatory over there,' she said, pointing across the terrace. 'I'm just going inside to pack a few things. I'll be out within ten minutes or so. Have the car turned round and ready to leave at a moment's notice.'

The young chauffeur looked baffled, but nodded. As she plunged her key into the lock and entered the house, Emma had a frantic, apprehensive flash of certainty that Richard would come in pursuit of her. She tried to tell herself that the fear was ridiculous. After all, it was hardly likely that Richard would drag himself away from his precious Amanda just to come and track his wife down. But if he did she didn't want to see him. She wanted to be away from here long before he arrived. Unfortunately, her foreboding was sound.

Most of her possessions were already packed, but she had just changed into a simple jersey suit and was stuffing more clothes into a suitcase when she heard the familiar sound of Richard's BMW hurtling down the drive. Springing to her feet, she slammed the suitcase shut, grabbed a coat and prepared to leave. But it was already too late. Richard was standing in the bedroom doorway, his breath coming in a shallow, rapid rhythm

as if he had just run up the stairs. His eyes were narrowed angrily and his whole body seemed to radiate
antagonism.

'What the hell do you think you're doing?' he growled,
prowling across the room to her with the tread of a jungle
cat.

'Leaving,' said Emma tersely.

'Oh, no, you're not. You're staying right here where
you belong.'

The suitcase in Emma's hand was becoming unbearably heavy and she flung it down with an angry
crash.

'You've got a hide, Richard!' she stormed. 'You think
you can just snap your fingers and I'll come running
back to you like a puppy, don't you? Well, I don't have
to take this kind of nonsense from you. I'm leaving!'

Unclenching her cramped fingers for a moment, she
made a snatch at the suitcase. But Richard was too quick
for her. He grabbed it away and held it out of her reach.

'Would you mind telling me why?' he demanded in a
low, menacing voice.

Emma gave a mirthless sneer of laughter.

'I would have thought even a towering intellectual
genius like my husband could have figured that out!' she
retorted. 'After all, wasn't that exactly what you wanted
me to do? Isn't that why you sent your girlfriend round
to me this morning with an airline ticket?'

Richard looked stunned.

'What are you talking about?' he demanded.

Emma rummaged inside the handbag which was
hanging from her shoulder and brandished the red
document at him.

'This! Your precious Amanda brought it round this
morning.'

'She's not my precious Amanda,' snarled Richard.

'Oh, pull the other leg, Richard, it's got bells on.'

'Look, Emma, Amanda is not my girlfriend! And I know nothing about this bloody airline ticket. What I do know is that you've been acting like a spoilt prima donna ever since yesterday.'

'Prima donna? *Prima donna*?' shrieked Emma. 'All right, so I'm a prima donna because I don't like my husband bringing his mistress home to my house!'

'She is not my mistress,' said Richard through his teeth.

Emma fought hard to control her ragged breathing.

'Oh, isn't she? Then why did you tell me you were thinking of marrying her?'

Richard ground his teeth.

'To make you jealous! Amanda and I have been professional colleagues until now, never anything more, I swear it.'

Emma flashed him a cold, incredulous look.

'Then why was she in my sitting-room telling you that she loved you yesterday?'

Richard's face took on a hunted expression. He ran his fingers through his tousled, curly hair in a baffled gesture.

'Apparently she's been carrying a torch for me for the last two years,' he said in a quieter voice. 'I had no idea about it until she came to see me yesterday. She spilled out all this nonsense about being in love with me. But I've never done anything to encourage her. Truly.'

His voice held such raw sincerity that Emma wavered with a tormented expression on her face. Then she looked down at her own wrist and saw that she was still wearing the gold and ruby bracelet that had caused so much trouble between them in the past. At once the whole agonising episode of the Blue Mountains came hurtling vividly back to her.

'I don't believe you,' she said coldly. 'It's just as it was in the first year we were married. You're such a smooth operator, Richard, that I never even know when you're lying. I would never have known that you were taking that other woman off to the Blue Mountains if you hadn't lost my bracelet there.'

'Blue Mountains? Bracelet?' echoed Richard in a baffled voice. 'What are you talking about, Emma?'

'This,' cried Emma.

With an angry gasp she unfastened the catch, wrenched the piece of jewellery off and flung it at him. Instinctively, he fielded it and stared down at his palm with a baffled expression.

'It's the bracelet you showed me yesterday. Is there something special about it?'

By now Emma's heart was hammering so violently that she could feel the blood pounding in her ears and her breath was coming in long, dragging gulps.

'You don't even remember. You bastard! You bastard! All right, I'll refresh your memory. After we had that quarrel about whether my father deliberately made you go broke, you stormed out in a huff and stayed away for five days. Didn't you?'

'That's true,' agreed Richard warily.

'Right,' continued Emma, gaining speed. 'And while you were gone you took some other woman up to the Blue Mountains for a weekend.'

'Where did you get this nonsense?' demanded Richard in an enraged voice.

'It's not nonsense! It's true. What made it even worse, you gave her my bracelet. My bracelet that was my father's gift to me on my eighteenth birthday! I hardly ever wore it because it was too ornate but it still had sentimental value. You were the only one who knew that and you gave it away to somebody else.'

'Emma, you're losing your mind,' said Richard patiently. 'It never happened.'

'It did!' Emma stamped her foot. 'What you hadn't planned on was that your little fluffball would lose the bracelet in the motel you stayed at. The Norfolk Pines Motor Inn. The manager phoned me the next day and told me the maid had found it under the double bed while she was cleaning the room. I was mystified. I told him it couldn't be mine because I hadn't been there. He read me back the details from the register. Mr and Mrs Richard Fielding, 968 Cross Street, Woolloomooloo had stayed there the previous night. My address, my name! You took somebody else there posing as your wife and gave her my bracelet and you thought I'd never even miss it.'

'Like hell I did! I've never stayed in the Blue Mountains in my life.'

'Richard, I went up there and identified the bracelet! I had insurance photos to prove it was mine! If you're going to lie to me, you've got to do better than that.'

Richard stepped back a couple of paces and looked down at the bracelet in his hand with a stunned expression.

'I don't understand. I spent the whole five days after I walked out of our place on the telephone at my sister Christina's flat, trying to organise a bridging loan so I wouldn't go broke. I didn't have time to breathe, let alone seduce some mythical woman.'

Emma's voice was heavy with sarcasm.

'So I suppose you'll say next that you didn't have time to read my letter, won't you, darling?' she demanded.

'Letter?'

'Don't give me that, Richard! Don't lie and twist things and pretend you never received it. I gave it to my father to hand deliver and he swore he found you in your office and gave it to you.'

'Did he now?' said Richard softly. 'And what did it say, Emma?'

Emma tried twice to speak and failed. She knew the letter by heart, but at first she could not force herself to say the words aloud. At last she spoke in a flat, expressionless voice that robbed them of all emotion. 'Dear Richard, I'll never understand why you had to turn to another woman and it breaks my heart to think of it. All the same, I love you. I can't bear to live without you. Please come back and make a fresh start with me. Please, please, please. Emma.'

Richard passed his hand over his brow.

'You wrote that? You thought I betrayed you and you still wrote that to me?'

Emma choked back a low, hoarse sob.

'Stupid, wasn't it? That was back in the days when I believed in love and happy endings. I was such a fool!'

'Don't say that,' urged Richard, taking a step towards her.

She backed away like a cornered animal.

'I will say it! I was a fool to think love would change anything. I loved you, Richard, I loved you so much I could hardly bear it. When I found out you'd been unfaithful to me, even then I wouldn't give up, but swallowing my pride and begging didn't bring you back, did it?'

Richard shook his head in a dazed fashion.

'I don't understand half of this, Emma,' he said. 'But I do know one thing. It's not too late for us.'

'Yes, it is!' shouted Emma. 'I don't care what you say, Richard, I'm quitting. I'm going as far away as possible and I'm going to start a new life with my child.'

The colour drained out of Richard's face. He stood completely motionless as though he had been frozen to the spot.

'Did you say your child?' he breathed.

'Yes, Richard,' she hissed. 'And since it's your child, too, I suppose I'll eventually have to grant you access to it, but don't expect me to have any more to do with you than I can possibly help. If I had my way, I'd never set eyes on you again as long as I live. Well, I guess this is goodbye. I hope you and Amanda will be very happy!'

Her sudden lunge took him off guard. Not even bothering to grab her suitcase, she ran for the stairs.

'Emma, come back!' he roared.

Not likely, she thought, hurtling down them at breakneck speed. I've got my passport, my ticket and my traveller's cheques right here in this bag and I don't need anything else from you. Ever.

Blundering through the sun-room in the dark, she reached the conservatory door and fumbled at the key with frantic, clumsy fingers. A moment later and she had pulled it softly closed behind her. A quick dash through the scented, leafy darkness between the rows of plants and her fingers closed again on another door-handle. This time it was the outside door. She emerged into the fitful shadows where the limousine stood waiting and wrenched open the back door of the vehicle. Collapsing into the back seat, she took a long, unsteady breath.

'Take me to the airport,' she ordered.

CHAPTER NINE

THE palm trees rustled gently in the warm, tropical breeze and through the open doorway the sweet scent of frangipani drifted on the air. In the distance Emma could hear the muted sounds of laughter and splashes from one of the swimming-pools. Otherwise there was silence. Leaning forward, she picked up a wedge of pineapple from the luscious array of tropical fruits in front of her and began mechanically to eat. The fruit was juicy and sweet, but eating it was an effort—everything was an effort these days. Only the thought of the unborn child she carried inside her forced her to go through the motions of chewing and swallowing. Sooner or later she knew she would have to return to Sydney and confront Richard, deal with the pain of seeking a divorce. But for the present she was content to remain here in Bali, feeling as if she was in sanctuary, protected from the ugliness of the real world. In the three days since she had arrived here, she had scarcely even gone outside except to stroll on the moonlit beach at night and to swim in the pool early in the morning when there was little chance of having to talk to anyone else. One day she would have to begin putting her shattered life back together, but not now. Not yet. A sudden footfall sounded on the stone floor of the balcony outside and she glanced up to see a hotel employee standing beneath a swag of hanging crimson bougainvillaea. His even white teeth flashed in a hesitant smile and he knocked on the already open front door.

'Yes?' said Emma encouragingly.

He stepped forward.

'Your car for Penelokan is ready, madam. The driver is here,' he chanted, as if repeating a lesson learnt by heart.

Emma gave him a mystified frown.

'There must be some mistake,' she began. 'I didn't order—— '

'I will bring him, madam,' promised the bellboy.

He scuttled out of sight among the shrubbery and a moment later a new figure stepped into view. A tall, blond man with a muscular physique and the most vivid, searing blue eyes Emma had ever seen in her life. A current of disbelief flared through her entire body as she watched him stride up the stairs with the bellboy in his wake carrying two suitcases.

'Richard,' she breathed.

Without taking his eyes off her, Richard stepped inside the bungalow, tipped the bellboy and ushered him off the premises. Then he calmly shut the door and turned to face her. Her first involuntary surge of delight gave way to panic and alarm. She retreated across the room and stared at him coldly.

'Go away, Richard,' she gabbled. 'I have nothing to say to you.'

Ignoring her words, he advanced on her with an urgent, burning light in his eyes. Then suddenly he caught her by the arms and gazed down at her earnestly.

'But I have something to say to you,' he said in a low, hoarse voice. 'And it's this. I love you, Emma. I've never stopped loving you. I want you to come back as my wife. And this time it's genuine.'

Her green eyes flicked sceptically up to meet his.

'Is this because of the baby?' she asked.

'No, it's not because of the baby! It's because of you. I can't bear to live without you.'

Her face contorted at the words she had once longed to hear. But she had been through too much disillusionment to believe them.

'That's nice,' she said in a brittle voice. 'But I can't bear to live with you. And I'm not prepared to share you with Amanda.'

Richard swore under his breath.

'You don't have to,' he insisted. 'I've never made love to Amanda in my life. Anyway, she's on her way to New York now with a fat severance payment. Once I found out how she had telephoned you from Gosford and visited you at our house, I told her she'd have to leave. I couldn't allow her to go on telling you such appalling lies and hurting you so much.'

Emma stiffened and stared up at him suspiciously.

'Lies? What do you mean, Richard? Are you telling me you didn't spend the night in Gosford with her?'

Richard gave a short laugh.

'Oh, yes, I did. But we were knee-deep in black coffee and legal documents the entire time. There wasn't a candlelit dinner or a feather bed in sight. And I had no idea that she telephoned you about it. Heaven knows I tried often enough, but the phone seemed to be off the hook the entire night.'

'B-but the airline ticket, the divorce settlement she offered me——' Emma stammered.

Richard scowled.

'Amanda's always had a shrewd sense of bluff,' he said curtly. 'She was only trying to frighten you off and leave the way clear for herself. She admitted as much when I went to her home and tackled her about it the day after you left Sydney. But she was wasting her time, Emma. I've never been interested in another woman from the first moment I laid eyes on you.'

There was so much harsh sincerity in his voice that a lump rose in her throat. She had to force herself to remember the incident which had caused their marriage to break up years before.

'The Blue Mountains——' she began.

'I've never been to the Blue Mountains in my life!' growled Richard. 'But I've been doing some detective work in the last few days and I've found out now what did happen. It was all a put-up job by your father to drive us apart. And he succeeded too, damn him! If I'd had the slightest suspicion what he was up to, I would have flattened him. But I never guessed and neither did you.'

'Guessed what?' asked Emma in bewilderment.

Richard broke away from her and prowled angrily across the room before turning back to face her.

'Frank never liked me and he had cooked things up to make it look as though I was being unfaithful to you. But it was a total fabrication, Emma. Look at this.'

Snatching open one of the bags on the floor, he rummaged inside and produced a handful of documents. Unclipping a photocopy from the top, he handed it to her.

'It's a Visa Card statement,' she said in a baffled voice.

'Yes. I got it from Miss Matty. She had every record of Prero's going back to the year dot. Just look at the date. December the twenty-second, over eight years ago. The Visa Card is in your father's name, so can you tell me why he was paying for one night's accommodation in the Norfolk Pines Motor Inn in the Blue Mountains for Mr and Mrs Richard Fielding when neither you nor I was anywhere near the area at that time? Suspicious, isn't it? And didn't good old Frank have access to the bracelet I'm supposed to have given to this woman? Couldn't he have planted it at the motel and arranged for the manager to phone you about it?'

Emma went chalky white as the pieces of the puzzle began to drop into place.

'Dad wouldn't——' she began hotly. And then stopped. Wouldn't he? Would a man who had snatched his two-year-old daughter away from her mother really hesitate to come between husband and wife? Suddenly Miss Matty's words rang in her head. 'Mr Prero could be very unpleasant if you crossed him, very vindictive.' She stared in horror as the uncomfortable suspicion grew.

'He would,' insisted Richard grimly.

Emma felt as if her legs had given way beneath her. Gripping the arm of the couch for support, she sat down, shaking her head. Quite suddenly she found Richard on the couch beside her, with his massive arms protectively around her. He gazed down at her with a compassionate expression.

'There's worse,' he warned. 'But you ought to know the truth. Your father destroyed the letter you wrote to me asking me to come back. He got Miss Matty to put it through the shredder in her office.'

Emma gasped.

'Miss Matty wouldn't do something so cruel to me!' she protested.

'She didn't know she was being cruel. Frank told her you'd changed your mind about sending the letter because you'd discovered that I was still being unfaithful to you. She thought she was destroying it at your wish.'

There was no mistaking the bitterness in his tone. Emma stared at him with slowly dawning comprehension, suddenly realising that he was innocent of the offences she had blamed him for all these years. There had been no reason to hate him and distrust him, no reason at all!

'O-oh, heavens! I'm so sorry, Richard,' she stammered. 'You mean you never did sleep with somebody else, you never did ignore my letter?'

He shook his head.

'No. All I did was lose my temper, tell you your father was an unscrupulous old bastard and storm out of the house. And the only things I did while I was away were to raise a loan to save my business and uncover further rumours that Frank had tried to ruin it in the first place.'

'You really believe he did that to you?'

'Oh, yes. He was as mean as they come. I never had hard evidence before, but I've got documents now to prove it. He deliberately tried to make me go broke, and all because I had dared to fall in love with you and marry you.'

Emma closed her eyes briefly and shuddered.

'And I...nearly had an affair with Nigel,' she breathed. 'Oh, Richard, can you ever forgive me?'

A stormy light flickered in his blue eyes and he grimaced.

'I won't pretend it thrills me, even now. But how could I not forgive you, Emma? You believed I'd been unfaithful to you, that I had ignored your generous attempt to patch things up and that I had made no effort to contact you... I don't suppose you ever received the dozen red roses I sent you on our first wedding anniversary?'

She shook her head in anguish. No, by then she had been living back in her father's house. No doubt he had made sure she never received them!

'Frank again,' breathed Richard. 'Of course. So there you were, twenty years old, hurt, bewildered and ripe for seduction by the man your father favoured...'

Emma gave a muffled groan.

'Oh, Richard, I've never regretted anything so much in my life!' she exclaimed. 'But I was so unhappy. I tried to convince myself that I loved Nigel, but deep down I knew it wasn't true. You didn't seem to love me any more and I wanted to hit back... But when he asked me to sleep with him—I just couldn't.'

'Whereas the truth is that I never stopped loving you.'

'But those other women...' she said uneasily.

He scowled.

'There were no other women until a long time after we split up. Perhaps three years later.'

'But you admitted that you were involved with other women while you were still married to me...'

'I've been married to you for the last nine years, Emma,' Richard reminded her. 'Married legally and in my heart. I kept hoping you'd come back to me. When you didn't, I eventually tried to blot you out by turning to other people. But it didn't work. I could never forget you.'

'I could never forget you, either,' admitted Emma huskily. 'After I left Nigel, I just lived for my work. There was nothing else in my life.'

'You left Nigel?' asked Richard.

'Yes.'

'Why?' he demanded.

'Because he wasn't you,' she said simply.

'And those other men——'

'There were no other men. You know the journalists, Richard. Some of them don't believe in messing up a good story with the facts.'

Richard winced.

'I know. My exploits weren't half as colourful as they were made out to be either. In the end I got thoroughly sick of that kind of life myself. All I wanted was for you to come back to me, but you never did. And then one day I heard the major tenant for your new office block had gone broke and Prero's was likely to follow suit. I saw my chance to get you back, so I followed you here to Bali and put my proposal to you.'

Emma screwed up her face in bewilderment.

'But if you still loved me, why didn't you just ask me to come back to you genuinely?' she demanded.

Richard ran his fingers through his wild blond curls and sighed.

'Wounded pride,' he admitted. 'A masculine thirst for revenge. Don't forget my view of what had happened, Emma. As far as I knew, you'd simply upped and left me because I'd insulted your precious father. And to add insult to injury you'd gone off with Nigel almost at once. Even after your father died and you and Nigel split up, my rage never really cooled. I wanted to drag you off by the hair and force you to admit that I was the better man.'

A dimple began to appear in Emma's cheek.

'I see,' she said evenly.

Richard glared at her.

'Then I wanted you to crawl on your hands and knees and admit that you'd made a mistake in leaving me,' he continued. 'I wanted you to say that you still loved me.'

'But I did!' protested Emma. 'At Air Panas. That first night we made love. And you flung my words right back in my face.'

Richard groaned.

'I know. It was because you said it too soon. I couldn't believe it was real. One night, and you were turning to melted butter in my arms? It seemed too suspicious to be true. I thought it was some kind of game you were playing or something you said to every man you were involved with. I was wild with jealousy and I felt my whole carefully laid plan was crumbling to dust right at the beginning.'

'"Carefully laid plan",' echoed Emma thoughtfully. 'Richard, what was your plan? Did you seriously intend just to stay with me for three months and take your revenge, then walk out on me?'

'I don't know any more!' he admitted with a mirthless laugh. 'I certainly told myself I did. But I soon realised I couldn't go through with it. I'd been eight years away from you and then, after only one night of making love with you, I was right back where I started—needing you, loving you, hating you! Ready to worship the ground you trod on. I couldn't handle it.'

'Is that why you were so hateful to me?' asked Emma.

'Yes,' he rasped.

'And why you let me think you were involved with Amanda?'

'Yes, again. It seemed like a heaven-sent camouflage for my true feelings, although I didn't know she fancied me herself at that stage. As time went by, I realised that what I was doing was ridiculous. I couldn't deny any longer that I loved you and I had to have you back. But for a long time my pride wouldn't allow me to come right out and say it to you. Somehow the words always stuck in my throat.'

'But that day I walked in on you and Amanda at home she was telling you that she loved you. Why didn't you——?'

'I wanted to do the decent thing by both of you,' he broke in irritably. 'She seemed genuinely upset and I tried to calm her down and get rid of her so that I could talk to you. But you wouldn't listen, even when I shouted through the bedroom door that I loved you.'

Emma flashed him a swift, guilty smile.

'I couldn't hear you. I had the Wagner turned up too loud.'

'I'll never listen to that vile CD again!' vowed Richard.

'No, you won't,' agreed Emma. 'I threw it in the trash.'

'You what?' roared Richard, momentarily diverted. 'You threw my Wagner CD in the trash?'

It sounded as if they were getting revved up for one of their shouting, stormy quarrels about nothing. Coming on top of the harrowing discoveries which had just shaken her to the core, it was too much for Emma.

A joyful, bubbling sense of relief surged through her and she burst out laughing.

'Oh, what does it matter?' she cried, throwing herself into Richard's arms and hugging him. 'What does any of it matter now that we're back together and it's all sorted out?'

He looked momentarily startled. Then, taking advantage of the opportunity presented to him, he cupped her face in his hands and kissed her with a passion and intensity that enthralled her.

'You have a point,' he admitted at last, gazing down at her through smoky, half-closed eyes. 'There's only one thing that matters now.'

'What's that?' asked Emma, nestling against him.

'That you're my wife and I love you now and forever. Will you come back to me, Emma? Properly this time? Permanently?'

'Of course I will!' she agreed fervently.

He dragged her against him with a growl of triumph. Suddenly all the tension between them was dissipated, transformed into a riotous, exuberant mood of rejoicing. Hauling her off the couch, he swung her bodily off the ground and into the air, then set her down and kissed her. And kissed her. And kissed her.

'You're never going to leave me again,' he vowed. 'In fact, you're going to spend a large proportion of your time gorgeously naked while I make violent love to you. Starting right this minute.'

Rising to his feet, he swept her off the couch into his arms and made for the stairs at a run. He was not even breathing heavily when he reached the bedroom upstairs, dropped her in the middle of the bed and gazed down at her with a long, appreciative look.

'Do I have any say in this?' mocked Emma.

'No,' replied Richard coolly, leaping astride her and untying the halter-neck of her dress. 'Kindly remember your place, woman. This marriage is not a democracy, it's a tyranny.'

'I see,' murmured Emma as Richard peeled the dress right off her and cupped her soft breasts in his hands. 'And the tyrant is about to have his evil way with me, is he?'

'Mmm,' agreed Richard, caressing her provocatively. 'Want to scream for help?'

'Help!' squeaked Emma softly. Then she raised her mouth to his. 'Oh, damn, no sign of rescue! Looks as though I'm out of luck. I guess I'll just have to give in. Oh, Richard... Oh, Richard! Do that again!'

He rose to his feet and in a few frantic movements had stripped off his clothes, tearing his shirt in the process. Then suddenly he was warm and hard and naked beside her, letting his hand trail over her flanks in a tender, appreciative caress. Emma sighed rapturously.

'Are you sure this won't hurt the baby?' he demanded between kisses.

She smiled mischievously.

'The doctor said it was all right.'

His lips touched her ear.

'I'm so proud, so thrilled to think that you're carrying my child,' he murmured. 'It's almost the best thing of all. But not quite. The best thing of all is being back together. Being man and wife.'

His hand continued to stroke her in a way that was provocative, intimate, wildly arousing. Soon she was gasping, twisting under his touch, reaching for him so that she could return the pleasure he was giving her. And when her whole body was a heated, throbbing ferment of love and need he entered her at last and brought her to a climax so thrilling that she turned her face into his shoulder and cried out. Through the warm, thundering waves of fulfilment that were breaking over her, she heard the distant sound of his voice.

'I love you, Emma. I love you, I love you, I love you.'

'I love you too, Richard,' she whispered hoarsely.

Hours later, when they had slept and eaten and showered and loved again, he pulled her to her feet and announced that they were going out. Giggling weakly, she allowed him to manhandle her back into her clothes.

'I can't be bothered,' she protested. 'I want to stay here in a state of ecstasy forever. Where are we going anyway?'

'Penelokan.'

That silenced her. Penelokan, where they had made their vows of undying love on their honeymoon. And, even if Richard couldn't remember what he had said to her, at least he knew it was a magical, special place for both of them. Yes, it was fitting that they should return there.

A late tropical shower had fallen while they were in bed and every bush and tree along the road gleamed with the rainbow light of a thousand diamond droplets. On the muddy roadside verges huge, fresh puddles reflected a dazzling blue sky and, when Emma rolled down the window, a surge of moist, flower-scented air wafted into the car. Pagodas and village compounds glided by and thickets of rainforest and rice paddies and flocks of quacking white ducks. Then they began their ascent into the mountains and the air grew as cool and potent as chilled white wine. At last they came through the great moss-encrusted ceremonial stone gateway and found the mountain country laid out before them in a vivid panorama of emerald-green and blue. Stopping the car, Richard helped her out. They were at Penelokan.

The view from the look-out was as spectacular as ever with Mount Batur rearing up in the background and the lake lying like a jewel among the rolling green hills. As Emma stood gazing down at it, she could not help feeling a brief pang of nostalgia for the moment they had shared here on their honeymoon and the words Richard had spoken to her then. But what really counted was that his arm was warm and powerful around her, that she could hear the steady beating of his heart and that he loved her to the depths of his soul. What did words matter, after all?

Then suddenly Richard drew her to him and looked down into her eyes with an intent, brooding expression on his face. She gazed back at him with a questioning look.

'Emma Fielding,' he said quietly. 'I swear I'll love you until that mountain is levelled and that lake runs dry.'

An incredulous joy soared through her entire body, so that she felt she could take wings and fly.

'R-Richard!' she stammered. 'You remembered?'

'How could I ever forget?' he murmured.

And his mouth came down on hers.

Especially
for you
on
Mother's Day

**Four new romances for just £5.99—
that's over 20% off the normal retail price!**

We're sure you'll love this year's Mother's Day Gift Pack–
four great romances all about families and children.

The Dating Game · Sandra Field
Bachelor's Family · Jessica Steele
Family Secret · Leigh Michaels
A Summer Kind of Love · Shannon Waverly

Available: February 1995   Price: £5.99

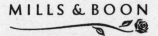

MILLS & BOON

Temptation

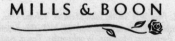

Lost Loves

'Right Man...Wrong time'

All women are haunted by a lost love—a disastrous first romance, a brief affair, a marriage that failed.

A second chance with him...could change everything.

Lost Loves, a powerful, sizzling mini-series from Temptation starts in March 1995 with...

**The Return of Caine O'Halloran
by JoAnn Ross**

MILLS & BOON

"All it takes is one letter to trigger a romance"

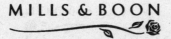

GET 4 BOOKS
AND A MYSTERY GIFT

Return the coupon below and we'll send you 4 Mills & Boon romances absolutely FREE! We'll even pay the postage and packing for you.

We're making you this offer to introduce you to the benefits of Reader Service: FREE home delivery of brand-new Mills & Boon romances, at least a month before they are available in the shops, FREE gifts and a monthly Newsletter packed with information.

Accepting these FREE books places you under no obligation to buy, you may cancel at any time, even after receiving just your free shipment. Simply complete the coupon below and send it to:

HARLEQUIN MILLS & BOON, **FREEPOST**, PO BOX 70, CROYDON CR9 9EL.

NO STAMP NEEDED

Yes, please send me 4 Mills & Boon romances and a mystery gift as explained above. Please also reserve a subscription for me. If I decide to subscribe I shall receive 6 superb new titles every month for just £11.40* postage and packing free. I understand that I am under no obligation whatsoever. I may cancel or suspend my subscription at any time simply by writing to you, but the free books and gift will be mine to keep in any case.
I am over 18 years of age.

1EP5R

Ms/Mrs/Miss/Mr _____

Address _____

_____

_____ Postcode _____

mps MAILING PREFERENCE SERVICE

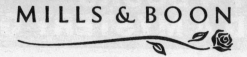

MILLS & BOON

Next Month's Romances

Each month you can choose from a wide variety of romance with Mills & Boon. Below are the new titles to look out for next month.

THE HEAT OF PASSION	Lynne Graham
SWEET SINNER	Diana Hamilton
UNWANTED WEDDING	Penny Jordan
THE BRIDE IN BLUE	Miranda Lee
FAITH, HOPE AND MARRIAGE	Emma Goldrick
PS I LOVE YOU	Valerie Parv
PARTNER FOR LOVE	Jessica Hart
VOYAGE TO ENCHANTMENT	Rosemary Hammond
HOLLOW VOWS	Alexandra Scott
DISHONOURABLE SEDUCTION	Angela Wells
TEMPTATION ON TRIAL	Jenny Cartwright
TO TAME A TEMPEST	Sue Peters
POTENT AS POISON	Sharon Kendrick
SHORES OF LOVE	Alex Ryder
DANGEROUS ATTRACTION	Melinda Cross
PASSIONATE RETRIBUTION	Kim Lawrence

Available from WH Smith, John Menzies, Volume One, Forbuoys, Martins, Woolworths, Tesco, Asda, Safeway and other paperback stockists.